CURSED BONDS: A FATE ENTWINED

RIYA MATTOOS

To Mom, the anchor of my life—strict and unyielding on the surface, yet overflowing with a love so deep it nurtures my soul. Your sacrifices and unwavering support have been the quiet force behind everything I've achieved.

To Dad, the silent guardian with a heart full of love and hope, whose strength carries me in ways words cannot touch. Your belief in me, even in my weakest moments, has been my greatest source of courage.

To Rishab, my little star, the joy and laughter that brightens my world. You are not just my brother but my greatest gift—the one who makes me believe in the beauty of simplicity and innocence. Your presence fills my life with warmth, and you remind me every day what it means to truly love.

To Ronak, the one who defies definition, yet remains family in every way that matters, a silent strength I hold close.

To Zephen, the friend who became my savior in a time of despair. When I stood on the edge, ready to give up, you pulled me back with your unwavering strength and compassion. You guided me through my 10th boards, replacing fear with resilience, and reminded me that life could be faced with courage. Your impact on my life is a debt I can never repay.

To Ahmad, my best friend, my other self, the one who understands me in ways no one else ever could. You see through my chaos, my fears, and my silence, solving my problems as if they were your own. You are my mirror, my anchor, and my safe space—my constant in this ever-changing world. With you, even the heaviest burdens feel lighter, and the darkest days hold a glimmer of hope.

To Govind, who grew from a neighbor and tuition buddy into a steadfast friend, always steady and true. You are the quiet strength I could always count on, a bond that time and distance could never weaken.

To Shivam, the one friendly face in the storm who traveled miles just to be there for me. When I was completely stuck, you showed up with unwavering courage and kindness, proving that true friendship knows no distance or hesitation. I'll never forget what you did for me.

To Sabrina, the sister I never expected but found in the most beautiful way. You became my protector and confidante, making me feel safe and never alone. Your care has been a gift I will always treasure.

To Abram, a steadfast presence whose quiet strength and support have been a source of comfort and peace—a true reminder of what it means to stand firm in love and loyalty.

To Nahal, a beacon of warmth and compassion, whose kindness lit the way through my darkest days—a soul who showed me the beauty of healing through gentleness.

To Mariam Hashir, a friend whose presence has been a constant light in my darkest hours. Your unwavering support and the warmth of your nightingale's voice have been a source of comfort and inspiration. Knowing I can count on you is a gift I deeply cherish.

To Ramya, my steadfast support system in a class where I often felt alone. Your kindness and unwavering presence turned an isolating space into one of comfort and understanding, and for that, I am deeply grateful.

To Aditi, who, despite being younger, cared for me like a mom and an older sister from the very first day we met. Thank you for listening to my endless venting and for keeping our bond strong—you've shown me what true love and patience look like.

To Omar and Hasil "Khan," brothers born not of blood but of shared struggles, who pulled me out of the deepest pits of despair. You didn't just stand by me—you fought my battles as if they were your own, proving that true family is forged in the fires of adversity.

To Mohammad, the older brother who stood like an unshakable wall, promising to protect me—and keeping that promise with every breath—a hero in every sense, whose unwavering care shaped my courage.

To Priyanka, Hiba, Nat, Shanoop, Fatema, Alaa and Atif—my unyielding sentinels of light during the darkest nights. Each of you, in your own unique way, has been a beacon of strength, pulling me back from the brink when shadows threatened to overwhelm. Your kindness and unwavering belief in me are treasures I will hold forever.

To Merly, a bond preserved like a delicate thread through the years. Your quiet support and unwavering loyalty have been a testament to the beauty of true friendship.

To Vishal, the friend who feels like an unspoken bond, an unnameable connection I trust without question, a quiet constant in my life—a silent strength that made every challenge bearable.

And to every friend whose name I may have missed but whose impact I never could—you are the quiet heroes in the background of my story.

To all of you—my heart, my foundation, my unbreakable bonds.
This story is yours as much as it is mine.

Contents

Foreword

I may not have known Riya for as long as some others, but I've come to realize that the depth of a connection isn't measured by the time you've spent together—it's about the impact someone has on your life. It's hard to believe that nearly three years have passed since our paths first crossed, yet in that time, you've become such an irreplaceable part of my life. You've inspired me in ways I didn't even think were possible, and I can confidently say that knowing you has made me a better person.

Riya, you truly are one of the strongest and most resilient individuals I've ever had the privilege of knowing. Life hasn't always been kind or easy, but you've faced every challenge with grace, courage, and a strength that leaves me in awe. Despite everything this messy world has thrown your way, you've stayed true to yourself—still that same kind, compassionate soul who lights up every room you enter. You have this incredible ability to make those around you feel seen, valued, and loved, and I can't tell you how much that means to me.

In my eyes, you are the very definition of a sweetheart. Your kindness is unwavering, your heart is pure, and your ability to remain so grounded in a world that often feels chaotic is nothing short of remarkable. Knowing you has been one of the greatest blessings of my life, and I feel endlessly lucky to call you my friend.

Thank you for being exactly who you are, Riya. Thank you for your patience, your laughter, your unwavering support, and your incredible spirit. I'm so proud of everything you've accomplished and the person you continue to be. Here's to many more years of friendship, love, and shared memories. You mean more to me than I could ever put into words.

With love,

Fatema S. N.

Preface

Every story has its shadows—moments of mystery, struggles, and the bonds that pull us through. *Cursed Bonds: A Fate Entwined* is a journey through darkness and light, a tale of identity, courage, and the unyielding strength of friendship.

This book isn't just a story; it's a reflection of something deeply personal. I've been fortunate enough to have friends who stood by me in my darkest of times in unimaginable ways. Their strength, loyalty, and unwavering presence shaped my own understanding of love and connection, even when the world seemed at its most uncertain.

Cursed Bonds: A Fate Entwined dives into those very themes—friendships tested by shadows, the secrets we carry, and the courage it takes to confront them. Reznor, Nocturne, and Hamoudi's story is one of hope in the face of despair, resilience in the face of doubt, and finding light in the places where darkness feels overwhelming.

This book is a love letter to the friends who become family, the ones who remind us that even in our most vulnerable moments, we are never truly alone. To anyone who has ever felt trapped by their own shadows, may this story remind you that light can always find its way in.

Thank you for walking alongside me on this journey. May the pages ahead leave an imprint on your heart as they did on mine.

— Riya Mattoos

Acknowledgements

This book would not have been possible without the love, guidance, and support of those who have played a vital role in my life.

To my family, for being my constant foundation and strength—thank you for your unconditional love and belief in me.

To my incredible teachers—Devi ma'am, Asha ma'am, Ayesha ma'am, and Sameena ma'am—your dedication and patience in helping me refine my language and expression have left an indelible mark on me. Thank you for shaping my skills and encouraging my growth.

To my friends, especially Zephen, Ahmad, Govind, Abram and Nahal—you have been my inspiration, my anchors, and my motivation in countless ways.

To my beta readers, editors, and all those who helped bring this story to life, your guidance and feedback have been invaluable.

Lastly, to anyone who supported this journey, whether directly or indirectly—thank you for believing in this story and in me.

With heartfelt gratitude,
Riya Mattoos

Prologue

The year was 1687, a time when shadows carried secrets and the air crackled with unspoken fears. Marguerite Delacroix, a woman of 27, lived in solitude at the edge of a village that whispered her name with both awe and suspicion. Her ivy-cloaked cottage was a place of mystery, nestled between the untamed forest and desolate moors. Known for her remedies and whispers of ancient incantations, Marguerite had always walked the fine line between healer and heretic. Yet, her power had never been wielded for selfish gain—until the night her desperation changed everything.

The tragedy began on a bitter January night when her three-month-old son, Philippe, teetered on the brink of death. Born too soon, his frail body was a pale imitation of the robust child Marguerite had envisioned. Her husband, François, had fled weeks earlier, unable to reconcile his wife's whispered abilities with his growing fear. Alone, Marguerite had poured her heart into saving her child—brewing potions, chanting words from her family's grimoires, and even seeking blessings from a God she no longer trusted. But nothing worked. Each breath Philippe took was a fragile gasp, and Marguerite knew his time was slipping away.

The moon hung high that night, its cold silver light cutting through the forest canopy as Marguerite carried Philippe into the heart of the woods. The clearing she sought was one she had only read about in the forbidden pages of her family's oldest tome—a place where the veil between this world and the next was said to be thin. Her arms cradled her dying son, her heart pounding with both fear and hope as she traced a circle into the frozen earth with a dagger etched with protective runes. She had no guarantees, only a mother's unyielding desperation.

Her voice trembled as she whispered the incantation, the ancient words slipping from her lips like a forbidden melody. The wind stilled, the air thickened, and a chill that seeped into her very soul settled over the clearing. Shadows began to twist and writhe at the edge of her vision, gathering into a form that was both formless and terrifying. When it spoke, its voice was a cacophony of whispers layered over each other, suffocating and undeniable.

"You dare summon me?" it hissed, its presence pressing down on her like the weight of the forest itself.

Marguerite's grip tightened around her son. "I have no choice. My son is dying. I will give anything—anything—to save him."

The entity laughed, the sound sharp and cold. "Anything, you say? Very well. A life for a life, Marguerite Delacroix. But understand this—no gift is without its price."

Before she could react, the shadows surged forward, wrapping around Philippe's tiny, lifeless form. Marguerite screamed as darkness seeped into her child's skin, his body convulsing once before stilling. For a moment, the clearing was silent, and then Philippe let out a cry—a strong, healthy wail that echoed through the night. Marguerite collapsed to her knees, sobbing as she clutched her son to her chest. He was alive.

But the entity did not leave. It lingered, its presence heavy and mocking. "Your son lives, but the cost is far greater than you know. Your bloodline is mine now, Marguerite. Every child born from your womb, every generation that follows, will carry my mark."

"No," Marguerite gasped, shaking her head. "That wasn't the deal!"

Its laughter reverberated through the clearing as it began to fade, leaving her words unanswered. The sigils carved into the ground glowed faintly before dimming, their power spent. Philippe had been saved, but at what cost?

François returned a week later, drawn by the news of his son's miraculous recovery. Yet, as soon as he saw Philippe—his eyes too bright, his movements unnaturally steady—he knew something was wrong. The boy's vitality was unnerving, almost otherworldly. The villagers' whispers grew louder, their glances sharper, and François's unease turned into dread. He confronted Marguerite, demanding answers she could not give, and when the omens began—the sudden death of livestock, the blight that destroyed their crops, and the eerie howls that echoed through the woods—François made his decision.

One cold morning, he left, abandoning his wife and child to the darkness that now seemed to follow them. His departure was a knife to Marguerite's heart, but she swallowed her grief and devoted herself entirely to Philippe.

Years passed, and Philippe grew into a strong, vibrant young man. The frailty of his infancy was a distant memory, replaced by a vitality that bordered on unnatural. He was faster, stronger, and sharper than any other boy in the village, a fact that only deepened the villagers' suspicion. Marguerite shielded him as best she could, insisting he was simply "special," but the truth lingered like a shadow in the corners of her mind.

At 20, Philippe married Éloise, a seamstress with a heart as kind as her smile. Their union brought a fleeting sense of normalcy to Marguerite's life, and when Éloise gave birth to a daughter, Amélie, Marguerite dared to hope that the curse would be forgotten. She doted on her granddaughter, finding solace in her bright laughter and innocent curiosity.

But the curse had not been forgotten. Philippe began to change, his temper growing shorter, his behavior more erratic. He spoke of voices in the forest, of dreams filled with shadows and whispers. Marguerite's heart sank as she recognized the signs—her son was succumbing to the darkness she had brought into their lives.

One fateful night, Philippe vanished. His body was found the next morning in the clearing where Marguerite had made her pact. His lifeless form lay in the center of a sigil carved into the earth, his face frozen in a mask of terror. Éloise, overcome with grief, fled the village with Amélie, vowing to protect her daughter from the shadow that had claimed her husband.

Marguerite, now 48 and weary from years of guilt, returned to the clearing one final time. She could not break the curse—its hold on her bloodline was too strong—but she could bind it, contain it until a descendant strong enough to face the entity could end it once and for all. With her blood, she carved the binding sigil into the earth, chanting the words of power that had haunted her dreams.

The forest trembled as the entity appeared, its anger palpable. "You think you can defy me, Marguerite Delacroix?"

She stood tall, her dagger gleaming in the moonlight. "I can. And I will."

The ritual completed, Marguerite collapsed to the ground, her life slipping away as the sigil glowed with a fierce light. Her final act of defiance sealed the curse to her bloodline alone, sparing others from its reach. When the villagers found her body the next morning, her face was serene, her sacrifice etched into the history of her family.

Her sacrifice had sealed the curse, but it had not destroyed it. Over the centuries, the Delacroix curse became a whispered legend, a tale of love, betrayal, and dark magic. Each generation bore its weight, their lives marked by tragedy and loss. And so, the curse lay dormant, waiting for the day when a descendant would rise to face the darkness and end its hold forever—Nocturne.

Nocturne had always felt it—an unsettling presence, like a shadow constantly trailing her, just out of sight. It wasn't something she could explain to anyone, not without sounding mad. The whispers in the dark, the strange dreams that left her waking in cold sweats, and the inexplicable bouts of anger and sorrow that would grip her without warning—these things had become a part of her life, though she couldn't understand why. Her parents had dismissed it as growing pains, just another phase in her tumultuous teenage years. But deep down, Nocturne knew it was something far more sinister, something ancient and waiting.

It wasn't until one summer afternoon, when the attic of her family's old farmhouse creaked with the weight of years, that Nocturne found the journal. Tucked away in a forgotten chest beneath piles of yellowing letters and cracked leather-bound books, the journal was a relic of her bloodline, its pages thick with age. The ink was faded, but the words jumped off the page with an energy that seemed to pulse through her fingers as she turned each brittle sheet. It was Marguerite's journal—the name that Nocturne had heard whispered only in the darkest corners of family stories. The more she read, the clearer it became: the curse had been passed down, dormant but alive, waiting for the right moment to awaken.

Nocturne's pulse quickened as the truth unfolded before her. The journal detailed Marguerite's pact with the entity, the promises made, and the sacrifices that had shaped her family's tortured history. It was as if the shadows themselves were speaking through the pages, telling Nocturne exactly what she had feared: the curse was real, and it had been waiting for her. Her strange dreams, her growing sense of otherness—it wasn't just her imagination. The darkness had always been a part of her. The grief, the anger, the odd moments of strength that seemed unnatural, they were all signs of the curse's grip on her bloodline.

As Nocturne delved deeper into Marguerite's tale, the weight of the curse settled over her like a suffocating fog. She saw the path her ancestor had walked, the desperation that had driven her to make a deal with something far more dangerous than any human could comprehend. The entity had come for her bloodline, drawing each generation into its grip, until Nocturne's time had arrived. Her heart pounded as she read about Marguerite's sacrifice, her final attempt to bind the curse to her descendants alone, hoping that one day, someone would be strong enough to end it. Nocturne knew that the curse had not been vanquished, only bound to the Delacroix family, its power waiting to rise again. And now, it was calling to her, drawn to her grief, her power, and the unyielding pull of her bloodline. The darkness had found her, and it was waiting.

CHAPTER ONE

A New World

Reznor Mortimer knew her name was strange. It wasn't the kind of name that let you slip quietly into the background. Teachers would hesitate during roll call, their brows furrowing slightly as if they were reading some ancient incantation. Classmates would give her sidelong glances or lean in close, whispering things they thought she couldn't hear.

"Reznor?" they'd ask, their voices laced with curiosity or ridicule. "Like... Trent Reznor?"

"Yeah," she'd mutter, pretending she didn't notice their confusion or the amused smirks that often followed.

Her dad loved the story behind her name, though. He told it at every opportunity, always with a sparkle in his eye. "Your grandma was a goth icon before the word even meant anything," he'd say, leaning back like he was spinning some legendary tale. "She had a thing for Nine Inch Nails. She thought Trent Reznor's music was pure poetry. When you were born, she convinced us to name you after him. Said it would be destiny."

Destiny. Reznor couldn't help but cringe whenever she heard the word. She didn't feel destined for much of anything, let alone something as intense and mysterious as her grandmother's world. She wasn't edgy or dramatic. She wasn't cool or bold. She liked pastel cardigans and cozy TV marathons. She liked comfort, predictability, and staying firmly in the safe zone.

But then, there was Veronica.

Or rather, there was Elvira.

They'd been best friends since first grade, back when Veronica had been just another bright, cheerful kid with a love for glitter and pop music. Together, they'd spent their childhood building pillow forts, choreographing dances to their favorite songs, and swapping secrets in whispers. But something shifted when high school rolled around.

At first, it was subtle. Veronica started wearing black. Then came the heavy eyeliner, the fishnets, and the spiked chokers. By sophomore year, she wasn't Veronica anymore.

"Call me Elvira," she announced one afternoon, her lips painted a deep crimson that matched her nails.

Reznor had laughed. "Elvira? As in Mistress of the Dark?"

"Exactly," Elvira said with a sly grin. "It suits me, don't you think?"

Reznor had shrugged, unsure what to say. It did suit her, in a way. The new name fit the sharp edges that Veronica had begun to embrace, the dark intensity in her eyes that hadn't been there before.

"Why goth, though?" Reznor asked one day as they lounged in Elvira's room, surrounded by posters of bands she didn't recognize.

Elvira twirled a strand of her newly dyed black hair around her finger. "Because it's real," she said simply. "It's not about pretending everything's fine when it's not. It's about looking at the darkness and saying, 'I'm not afraid of you.' You'd get it if you gave it a chance."

Reznor shook her head, laughing nervously. "Yeah, I don't think so. I'm not exactly goth material."

"You're wrong," Elvira said, her voice quiet but firm. "You just don't know it yet."

At the time, Reznor had brushed it off, but something about Elvira's words lingered. It wasn't until months later, when one of Elvira's playlists accidentally shuffled into her own, that Reznor felt the first crack in her carefully constructed world.

The song started softly, a slow, haunting melody that sent shivers down her spine. The vocals were raw, almost fragile, but there was strength beneath them—a quiet defiance that resonated deep within her.

By the time the chorus hit, Reznor felt like she couldn't breathe. It was as if the music had reached into her chest, pulled out every buried emotion she'd been too afraid to name, and laid it bare.

She replayed the song three times before falling asleep, the lyrics looping in her mind like a whispered secret.

It wasn't long before her curiosity grew into something more. By the time Elvira invited her to a goth club called Obsidian Veil, Reznor had already started exploring the edges of this strange, dark world.

"I don't have anything to wear," Reznor protested as they planned for the night.

Elvira grinned, pulling out a bag stuffed with clothes. "Don't worry. I've got you covered."

What followed was an hour-long transformation that felt like stepping into another life. Black lace, silver jewelry, combat boots that made her feel both powerful and slightly ridiculous. When Elvira finished applying the last touch of eyeliner, Reznor barely recognized the person staring back at her in the mirror.

"You look amazing," Elvira said, her voice brimming with pride. "See? I told you this was your destiny."

Reznor rolled her eyes but couldn't help the small smile tugging at her lips.

The moment they stepped into Obsidian Veil, Reznor felt like the air had been knocked out of her. The music was deafening, the bassline vibrating in her chest. The scent of incense mingled with the sharp tang of metal, and the dim lighting turned every shadow into something alive.

"This is insane," Reznor whispered, clinging to Elvira's arm as they wove through the crowd.

"In the best way," Elvira said, her grin practically glowing in the dark.

While Elvira disappeared into the chaos to greet some friends, Reznor found herself lingering by a corner, unsure what to do with herself. Her confidence had evaporated the moment they walked in, leaving her feeling exposed and out of place.

"You look lost," a voice said, low and lilting.

Reznor turned, her breath catching as she took in the girl standing beside her. She was tall and elegant, her long black hair cascading over her shoulders like liquid night. Her gray eyes were piercing, like they could see through every layer of Reznor's carefully guarded defenses.

"First time here?" the girl asked, a faint smile playing on her crimson lips.

"Yeah," Reznor said, her voice barely audible over the music.

The girl extended a hand. "I'm Nocturne."

Reznor hesitated, then shook her hand. "Reznor."

Nocturne tilted her head, her gaze softening. "Reznor," she repeated, as if testing the name. "That's... unique. But I like it. It suits you."

Reznor felt her cheeks flush. "Thanks. My grandma named me after Trent Reznor. She was a goth."

Nocturne's smile deepened, but there was no mockery in it—only understanding. "That's fate," she said simply.

They spent the rest of the night talking, their conversation weaving effortlessly between music, art, and life. Nocturne's voice was as captivating as her presence, each word carrying a quiet intensity that made Reznor want to hang onto every syllable.

"People think goth is about darkness," Nocturne said at one point, her eyes gleaming like polished steel. "And they're right—but it's not just darkness. It's about finding the beauty in it, about embracing what others are too afraid to look at."

Reznor nodded, her mind buzzing with thoughts she couldn't yet put into words.

By the time the night ended, Reznor felt like she'd stepped into an entirely new version of herself. The black lace, the heavy boots, the music—they all felt like pieces of a puzzle she hadn't realized she was solving.

"You were made for this," Elvira said as they climbed back into the car.

For once, Reznor didn't argue. Instead, she glanced at her reflection in the window, her lips curving into a small, uncertain smile.

"Maybe I was," she whispered.

As she lay in bed that night, staring at the cracks in her ceiling, Reznor couldn't stop thinking about Nocturne. There had been something magnetic about her, something that made the world feel a little sharper, a little more alive.

For the first time in her life, Reznor felt like she was standing on the edge of something extraordinary. And for the first time, she wasn't afraid to take the leap.

CHAPTER TWO

THE CURSED CHILD

Monday morning broke with an air of reluctance, the faint drizzle settling over the town like a melancholic veil. Reznor walked briskly toward school, her breath forming wispy clouds in the crisp air. The changes in her over the past few weeks were subtle yet profound, like the slow erosion of stone into something sharper, more defined.

Her wardrobe had darkened as though it mirrored her inner metamorphosis—blacks, deep purples, and smoky grays now dominated her closet. Her makeup, previously an afterthought, had become a ritual of self-expression: thick, kohl-lined eyes and lipstick shades that bordered on daring. Even her stride, once hesitant and meandering, had steadied. She walked with purpose now, though she wasn't quite sure what that purpose was.

Elvira was waiting for her by the lockers, her sharp eyes immediately scanning her friend from head to toe.

"Well, look at you," she drawled, propping herself against the cold metal. "My little baby bat is finally embracing her wings."

Reznor snorted, fumbling with the lock. "Don't start."

"I'm serious. There's something different about you. It's like Obsidian Veil lit you up from the inside."

Reznor paused for a moment, the memory of the club flashing vividly in her mind: the pounding bass, the heavy scent of clove cigarettes, the shadowy figures moving in rhythm to music that spoke of despair and rebellion. And then there was Nocturne—her piercing gray eyes cutting through the dark like a storm contained within a single glance.

"It kind of did," she admitted softly.

Elvira raised a brow, clearly intrigued, but let it go for now. "Well, don't let it make you late for Fenton's class again. I swear that man gets off on docking participation points."

As they walked toward class, Reznor's gaze swept across the cafeteria, her eyes instinctively seeking out one figure amidst the sea of familiar faces. It didn't take long to find her.

Nocturne sat alone in the farthest corner, her presence a quiet defiance against the chatter and chaos around her. She wore her usual black hoodie, though today the sleeves were pushed up, revealing thin, silver bracelets circling her wrists. Her headphones hung loosely around her neck, faint tendrils of music escaping from them, and her notebook lay open before her. She was drawing again, her pen moving fluidly across the page.

"There she is," Reznor muttered under her breath, nudging Elvira.

Elvira followed her gaze and stiffened, her teasing demeanor replaced by something almost somber. "Nocturne? Oh, Rez."

"What?"

"You've heard about her, haven't you? They call her The Cursed Child."

Reznor turned to her sharply. "That's absurd. She's just a girl."

"She's a Delacroix," Elvira murmured as though the name itself carried weight.

The name sounded vaguely familiar, like something whispered in passing, but Reznor couldn't place it. "And?"

Elvira sighed, glancing around before lowering her voice. "Her family's practically a gothic novel. That house of hers—old Victorian mansion, overgrown gardens, the whole nine yards. People say it's cursed. Every firstborn daughter in the Delacroix line...they don't live past thirty. Her mom didn't, and her aunt's the only reason Nocturne still has a roof over her head."

Reznor frowned. "You're basing this on rumors."

"Maybe," Elvira said, shrugging. "But you've gotta admit, there's something...off about her. People who get too close to Nocturne—bad things happen. Accidents, breakups, fights. You can't tell me that's just coincidence."

Reznor rolled her eyes, irritation prickling beneath her skin. "She's just...different. And maybe if people treated her like a person instead of some cursed artifact, they'd see that."

Elvira sighed but didn't argue further.

Ignoring the stares and whispers that followed her, Reznor crossed the cafeteria and slid into the seat across from Nocturne.

"Hey," she said, her tone casual despite the nervous flutter in her chest.

Nocturne looked up, her gray eyes widening slightly in surprise before softening. "Reznor." She pulled off her headphones, letting them rest around her neck. "Didn't expect to see you here."

"Thought I'd say hi," Reznor said with a shrug.

Nocturne's lips curved into a faint smile. "You're aware everyone's staring, right?"

Reznor glanced around, catching the curious and judgmental gazes of their peers. She met Nocturne's eyes with quiet defiance. "Let them. I don't care."

Nocturne studied her for a moment, something unreadable flickering in her gaze. "Brave," she murmured. "Or reckless."

"Either way," Reznor said, grinning, "I'm here."

As the days passed, their connection deepened. They swapped playlists in the library, shared headphones as they huddled in dimly lit corners, and talked about everything from obscure music genres to the weight of feeling like an outsider.

One evening, over dinner, Reznor found herself bringing up Nocturne and the club to her father.

"Obsidian Veil?" he repeated, setting down his fork. His brow furrowed, and his expression turned guarded. "That's a goth club, isn't it?"

"Yeah. Elvira and I went a few weeks ago. It was...different."

Her father leaned back in his chair, his gaze steady but unreadable. "And this friend of yours—Nocturne. She's from the Delacroix family?"

Reznor nodded, suddenly feeling defensive. "She's not what people say about her, Dad."

"I'm not saying she is," he replied carefully. "But that family has a history. Old money, tragedy, secrets...It's not the kind of thing people forget."

"She's not her family," Reznor insisted. "She's...different. And she's my friend."

Her father held her gaze for a long moment before nodding. "Just be careful, kiddo. Sometimes, the shadows people carry aren't their fault, but they can still touch you."

The first time Reznor saw Nocturne's house, she was struck by how alive it felt—alive with stories, secrets, and a history that seemed to cling to every stone. The Delacroix mansion stood at the end of a long, winding driveway, its Victorian architecture both beautiful and imposing. Ivy crept up the walls, its tendrils curling around intricate carvings that had weathered the passage of time. The stained-glass windows, framed by heavy curtains, glimmered faintly in the fading light.

"Home sweet home," Nocturne said dryly as they walked up the creaking steps of the wraparound porch. A rusted wind chime hung in one corner, swaying gently in the breeze.

Inside, the house was a strange mix of elegance and melancholy. The high ceilings and grand staircase spoke of wealth and grandeur, but there was an undeniable air of neglect. Dust clung to the corners of ornate picture frames, and the once-polished floors creaked beneath their weight.

The walls were lined with bookshelves, their contents ranging from leather-bound classics to worn paperbacks. An antique chandelier hung above the living room, its crystals catching the light in muted flashes.

"This is incredible," Reznor murmured, her eyes scanning the room.

Nocturne shrugged, her expression unreadable. "It's just a house."

As they settled onto the worn velvet couch, Reznor noticed a framed photograph on the coffee table. It was of Nocturne as a child, standing beside a woman with dark hair and striking gray eyes.

"Your mom?" Reznor asked softly.

Nocturne's jaw tightened. "Yeah. She died when I was eight. Heart failure."

"I'm sorry," Reznor said, her voice heavy with sincerity.

Nocturne gave a faint, bitter smile. "It's a Delacroix tradition. Firstborn daughters don't make it past thirty."

"What about your dad?"

"Not in the picture," Nocturne said flatly. "I live with my aunt now. She's...fine. Just busy."

Reznor hesitated, unsure how to respond. The weight of the house—the history, the loss, the loneliness—pressed against her chest.

"Let me show you something," Nocturne said suddenly, standing and motioning for Reznor to follow.

She led her upstairs to a room that felt entirely different from the rest of the house. It was smaller, cozier, with walls covered in posters of bands and abstract art. Sketchbooks and notebooks were scattered across the desk, and an electric guitar leaned against the corner.

"This," Nocturne said, gesturing to the space around her, "is mine. The only part of this house that doesn't feel like a museum."

"It's perfect," Reznor said, meaning it.

Nocturne smiled—a real, unguarded smile that lit up her face.

For the first time, Reznor felt like she was seeing the real Nocturne, not the girl shaped by rumors and whispers. And she knew, without a doubt, that their story was only just beginning.

CHAPTER THREE

SHADOWS AND SECRETS

Reznor had fallen into an unspoken rhythm with Nocturne, a dynamic that felt as though it had always been meant to exist. Their lunchtimes were spent tucked away in the farthest corner of the cafeteria, speaking in low tones about bands that most of their classmates had never heard of. Their afternoons often stretched into evenings at Obsidian Veil, a place that felt alive with the energy of kindred spirits. It wasn't just a club—it was a sanctuary for people like them, outsiders who had no desire to fit into the glossy, prepackaged version of "normal."

For Reznor, this connection was something she hadn't realized she was searching for until she found it. It gave her a sense of belonging she'd never truly felt before. And yet, not everyone in her life was convinced.

"She's intense," Elvira remarked one cloudy afternoon as they wandered through the cramped aisles of a thrift shop. The place smelled faintly of lavender sachets and worn leather, the kind of place that invited quiet reflection. Elvira's voice carried a note of hesitation, as if she wasn't quite sure she should be saying it.

Reznor sighed, running her fingers over a rack of black lace dresses. "What exactly do you mean by 'intense'? And don't try sugarcoating it."

Elvira shrugged, her fingers brushing against a beaded handbag. "I mean...I don't know. She's cool, but there's something about her. Like...you can't quite figure her out, and it's unsettling."

"She's different," Reznor said, her tone sharpening. "That doesn't make her a threat."

"I'm not saying she's a threat," Elvira replied, her eyes narrowing slightly. "I'm saying that maybe you should be careful. You don't really know her."

Reznor set her jaw, pulling a dress off the rack and holding it up against herself. "She's been nothing but good to me, El. Maybe if you actually got to know her instead of deciding you don't like her based on some vague 'vibe,' you'd see that."

Elvira didn't respond, and the silence between them lingered, stretching like a taut thread until the subject was dropped altogether.

The following weekend, Reznor found herself back at Nocturne's home—the towering Victorian mansion that seemed to exhale its own history. The Delacroix house, with its peeling wallpaper and faintly oppressive atmosphere, had become familiar in a way that felt oddly comforting. She didn't mind the way the shadows seemed to cling to the corners of the rooms or how the floorboards creaked no matter how softly she stepped. It was a house that felt alive, its presence a constant companion.

"You're here a lot these days," Nocturne said with a faint smile as she poured tea into two mismatched porcelain cups. Her movements were slow and deliberate, as though every action carried its own unspoken meaning.

Reznor leaned against the arm of the couch, her lips quirking into a smirk. "What can I say? The haunted mansion vibe really does it for me."

Nocturne handed her a cup, her expression softening. "It's nice, though. Having you around. It gets...quiet here sometimes."

Reznor took a sip of tea, the warmth of it spreading through her chest. "What about your aunt? Doesn't she keep you company?"

Nocturne's eyes flickered, the faint smile fading from her face. "She tries, I guess. But she's...not the kind of person who really connects with anyone. She's been through a lot."

Reznor frowned, setting her cup down on the worn coffee table. "Like what?"

Nocturne hesitated, her fingers tightening around the handle of her cup. The silence stretched between them, heavy with the weight of something unsaid. Finally, she spoke, her voice barely above a whisper.

"She thinks I'm the next cursed one."

Reznor blinked, caught off guard by the starkness of the statement. "Cursed?"

Nocturne nodded slowly, her gaze fixed on the swirling surface of her tea. "It's been that way since I was little. Bad things always seem to happen to people close to me. My mom, my sister, my best friend...they all died. And not in ways that make sense. My mom had a sudden heart attack at 35. My sister drowned in our own pool, even though she'd been swimming since she was five. My best friend—" She broke off, her voice cracking.

Reznor leaned forward, her heart twisting at the raw pain in Nocturne's eyes. "You don't have to keep going if you don't want to."

Nocturne shook her head, a bitter laugh escaping her lips. "No, you deserve to know. Claire—my best friend—was helping me with a project at school. We were up late working, and she decided to run to the convenience store for snacks. She never came back. They found her body the next day. It was a hit and run."

Reznor's stomach churned, the weight of the story settling heavily on her. "That's...horrible. I'm so sorry, Nocturne."

"It is horrible," Nocturne said, her voice hardening. "But what's worse is how everyone reacted. They didn't blame her killer. They blamed me. They said I was cursed, that I brought bad luck. And after a while...I started to believe them."

"No," Reznor said firmly, reaching out to place her hand over Nocturne's. "You're not cursed. You didn't make those things happen. Bad things happen to good people all the time—it doesn't mean you're responsible."

For the first time, Nocturne looked at her, a flicker of something vulnerable and fragile breaking through her usual composure. "You really think so?"

"I do," Reznor said, her voice unwavering. "And if anyone tries to tell you otherwise, they'll have to answer to me."

Nocturne let out a soft laugh, the sound like the first drop of rain after a long drought. "Thanks, Reznor. You don't know how much that means to me."

It was around this time that Hamoudi began to enter their lives. Unlike Nocturne, whose presence was immediate and magnetic, Hamoudi's arrival was subtle, like a ripple that gradually became a wave. He wasn't the kind of person who commanded attention, yet his quiet confidence made him impossible to ignore.

Born into a devout Muslim family, Hamoudi's life was one of balance. His grandfather had immigrated to the country decades ago, seeking opportunities that the old world couldn't provide. Hamoudi now lived with his parents, two brothers—one older, one younger—and a younger sister he doted on. His family was close-knit, but Hamoudi had always been the one to question things, to form his own opinions rather than blindly following tradition.

He had an uncanny ability to read people, a skill that often left others feeling both exposed and understood. "People wear masks," he told Reznor one evening as they sat outside Obsidian Veil. "Sometimes to protect themselves, sometimes to deceive. But if you watch closely, you can always see the cracks."

Hamoudi's interest in Reznor wasn't hard to miss. He began sitting closer to her in class, offering to help with assignments, and even braving the goth scene at Obsidian Veil despite sticking out like a sore thumb. His awkward attempts to blend in were almost endearing, though Reznor couldn't help but tease him for it.

"You've got an admirer," Nocturne remarked one night as Hamoudi stood awkwardly by the bar, clearly unsure of what to do with himself.

"He's trying too hard," Reznor said, though she couldn't hide the faint smile that tugged at her lips.

"Maybe," Nocturne said with a smirk. "But he's got good taste."

Reznor rolled her eyes but couldn't help smiling. She wasn't sure how she felt about Hamoudi yet, but his earnestness was endearing.

One evening, Hamoudi approached them outside the club, his hands shoved into the pockets of his leather jacket.

"Hey," he said, his gaze flickering between them. "Mind if I join you?"

Nocturne shrugged. "As long as you can keep up."

Hamoudi grinned. "I'll do my best."

The three of them spent the night talking and laughing, with Hamoudi quickly proving he could hold his own in their world. By the end of the night, Reznor felt like their little trio had solidified into something unbreakable.

Hamoudi's persistence paid off. Over time, he became an integral part of their dynamic, his analytical mind and sharp wit complementing their darker, more introspective personalities. The three of them spent more time together, their bond deepening with every passing day. Yet, even as their friendship grew, the strange occurrences surrounding Nocturne continued to escalate.

It wasn't just the way she seemed to thrive in darkness or the way her presence felt both comforting and unsettling. It was the way things happened around her—small, inexplicable things.

Like the time they were walking home from school, and a car swerved onto the sidewalk, narrowly missing them. Or the time a shelf in the library collapsed, scattering books everywhere, but none of them were hurt.

Reznor tried to brush it off as coincidence, but the incidents kept piling up.

One afternoon, as they sat in Nocturne's living room, Reznor finally decided to confront her.

"Nocturne," she began carefully, "do you ever feel like...weird things happen when you're around?"

Nocturne's expression darkened. "What do you mean?"

"I mean...things that shouldn't happen. Accidents, close calls. Stuff like that."

Nocturne looked away, her hands clenched in her lap. "I try not to think about it."

"Why not?" Hamoudi asked, his voice gentle.

"Because if I do, it feels real," Nocturne admitted. "And I don't want it to be real."

Reznor exchanged a glance with Hamoudi, then reached out to take Nocturne's hand. "Whatever it is, we'll figure it out together. You're not alone in this."

Hamoudi nodded. "We've got your back, Nocturne. No matter what."

Nocturne looked at them, her eyes brimming with tears. "Thank you," she whispered. "You don't know how much that means to me."

The trio became inseparable, their bond deepening with every passing day. They faced the world together, navigating the challenges of high school and the complexities of their own lives.

For the first time in years, Nocturne felt like she wasn't carrying her burdens alone. And for the first time ever, Reznor and Hamoudi felt like they'd found something worth fighting for.

But as the shadows around them grew darker, they knew their journey was just beginning.

CHAPTER FOUR

SECRETS BENEATH THE SURFACE

Reznor's life had become a strange dance between clarity and chaos. On the surface, everything appeared normal—lectures, assignments, fleeting interactions with classmates—while beneath, an undercurrent of something far darker and more inexplicable swirled around her. The intensity of her relationship with Nocturne, the unexplained bond between them, was both compelling and terrifying. Every day, it became harder to ignore the weight of it all, as if the universe itself had conspired to pull them together. Yet in moments of quiet reflection, Reznor felt the pressing weight of uncertainty, of a future where something monumental loomed, and she didn't know if she was ready for it.

It was in these moments of restless silence that the dreams began to feel more like a warning than mere fragments of her subconscious. Every night, without fail, Reznor found herself walking through a forest—a place so vivid, so full of sensation, that the line between waking and dreaming blurred into nothingness.

The forest was endless and alive, thick with ancient trees whose twisted roots seemed to claw at the earth beneath them, as if searching for something long lost. The bark of the trees was blackened and gnarled, twisted into shapes that defied nature, each tree like a sentinel to something older than time itself. The air was suffocating, thick with the weight of centuries, the mist curling around her feet as if it had a will of its own, pulling her deeper into the darkened woods.

Every step she took sent echoes through the silence, each footfall a harsh intrusion into the stillness that suffocated her. The mist clung to her skin, cool and damp, as if the very air had weight, pressing down on her, filling her lungs with a strange, metallic taste. There were no sounds here—not the rustle of leaves, not the call of birds, not even the wind. Just an overwhelming, suffocating silence that pressed against her mind, threatening to crush her under its stillness. And yet, despite the quiet, the forest was alive. It hummed with something ancient, a presence that watched her from the shadows.

At the heart of this forest stood Nocturne. Always.

She stood with her back to Reznor, her long, black dress swirling in the breeze, but somehow not moving, like a shadow woven into the fabric of the world. Her hair, dark as midnight, spilled over her shoulders, but there was something strange about it—something that made Reznor's chest tighten in unease. The way the shadows seemed to dance around her, as if Nocturne herself was part of the very darkness that surrounded her.

"Nocturne," Reznor called, her voice trembling as it broke through the silence. But it felt wrong, as though the words were swallowed by the oppressive air, never truly leaving her mouth. It was as if the forest itself rejected her voice, turning her cries into mere echoes.

But Nocturne didn't respond.

Reznor took a step forward, then another, her breath quickening as she walked deeper into the forest. But no matter how much she moved, it felt as though she wasn't getting any closer to Nocturne. The trees seemed to shift around her, closing in on her, as though they had a mind of their own, blocking her path, twisting their limbs to hold her in place. The more she moved, the more distant Nocturne became, like a phantom forever out of reach.

"Nocturne!" Reznor cried again, her voice cracking, the desperation rising within her chest. Please, she thought. Why won't you speak to me?

Nocturne turned slowly, her face hidden in the shadows, her expression unreadable. Her eyes glowed faintly, like two silver flames burning in the darkness. There was something unsettling about her gaze, something ancient and mournful. And as she finally looked at Reznor, it was as though the forest held its breath. The air around them grew thick with tension, the world seeming to pause as if waiting for something.

"You shouldn't have followed me," Nocturne's voice was soft, but the words echoed as if they were coming from the very trees themselves. They stretched and warped unnaturally, reverberating in Reznor's mind, a cold and foreboding warning.

Reznor's pulse quickened. "Nocturne, please!" she cried, her feet moving forward, closing the distance. But with each step, the earth beneath her shifted, the ground pulling away from her, the roots of the trees rising from the soil to bind her. The more she tried to reach her, the more the forest fought against her. The roots twisted around her ankles, their grip like iron, dragging her into the earth, pulling her deeper into the suffocating soil, trying to bury her alive.

"Nocturne, please!" Reznor gasped, her heart pounding in her chest. "What's happening? What are you hiding from me? What is this place?"

Nocturne's silver eyes bore into hers, deep with sorrow and something far older, something far darker. This was never meant to be your burden, they seemed to say, though no words left her lips.

And then, as Reznor reached out to her, desperate, the dream shattered. The forest crumbled away like ash in the wind, and she was thrown into darkness, her breath coming in harsh gasps, her body drenched in sweat. She woke up in her bed, the remnants of the dream still clinging to her like a cold shroud, the echo of Nocturne's eyes still burning in her mind. But no answers came. Only more questions. And a creeping dread that something far more sinister than she could have imagined was happening.

One morning, unable to bear the weight of it alone, she brought it up while sitting with Hamoudi and Nocturne in the school courtyard.

"Do either of you have...weird dreams?" she asked, trying to keep her tone casual.

Hamoudi smirked. "Define weird. Are we talking falling-off-a-cliff weird or naked-in-class weird?"

"No," Reznor said, rolling her eyes. "Weird as in...too real. Like you're actually there."

Nocturne, who had been absently doodling in her notebook, froze mid-sketch. Her pencil hovered above the page as if caught between worlds. "Why are you asking?"

Reznor hesitated. "I've been having this dream," she admitted. "It's in a forest. You're there, Nocturne, but you're...different."

"Different how?" Nocturne's voice was barely audible.

"Your eyes. They glow."

For a moment, a heavy silence settled over them. Then, Nocturne closed her notebook with a snap and stood abruptly. "I need to go."

"Nocturne, wait!" Reznor reached for her, but she was already walking away, her long strides purposeful and final.

Hamoudi frowned. "What's her deal?"

"I don't know," Reznor said, her worry gnawing at her. "But I'm going to find out."

Reznor stood in front of Nocturne's apartment, the cold air biting at her skin. It wasn't just the chill of the evening that made her shiver; it was the weight of the unanswered questions. She had to know the truth. She had to understand what was happening to Nocturne—and to herself. The dreams, the strange connection, the unspoken tension that lingered between them all—it couldn't be a coincidence.

Her hand hovered in hesitation before she could knock, but the door creaked open on its own, its hinges groaning in protest. Reznor froze, her heart skipping a beat, the hairs on the back of her neck standing on end. She took a cautious step forward, peering into the dimly lit house.

The air inside was thick and oppressive, carrying the scent of burning candles mingled with something ancient and metallic—a sharp tang that made her skin crawl. Shadows danced on the walls, flickering and alive, cast by the scattered candles that surrounded Nocturne, who sat cross-legged on the floor. Her head was bowed, her raven-black hair spilling over her shoulders as her fingers traced the pages of an old, weathered book. The book seemed wrong, somehow, as if it didn't belong in this world. Its cover was cracked leather, worn with age, and its pages were yellowed, etched with symbols that defied logic.

"What is this?" Reznor asked, her voice barely above a whisper. The question hung in the heavy air, carried on her breath.

Nocturne didn't look up. Her focus remained on the book, her fingers trembling slightly as they moved across the strange markings. "I'm trying to understand," she murmured, her voice distant, like she was speaking to herself rather than to Reznor.

Reznor stepped further into the room, her unease growing with each step. The flickering candlelight illuminated the symbols on the pages—symbols that seemed to writhe and shift, as though they were alive. They were intricate, almost hypnotic, yet impossible to decipher. Her stomach twisted as she stared at them, a deep, primal part of her screaming that she shouldn't be here, that she shouldn't look.

"What's happening?" Reznor asked again, louder this time, her voice breaking the suffocating silence.

Finally, Nocturne looked up, her silver eyes meeting Reznor's. There was something in her gaze—sorrow, fear, and a depth of pain that made Reznor's heart ache. "The curse," Nocturne whispered, the words fragile, as though speaking them aloud might shatter her.

Reznor's breath hitched, the weight of those words settling over her like a lead blanket. "The curse?" she repeated, her voice trembling. "What do you mean?"

Nocturne closed the book with a soft thud, her hands lingering on its cover as if reluctant to let it go. "The Delacroix curse," she said, her voice tight. "It's real. I always thought it was just a story—a cruel, ancient myth meant to keep us in line. But... it's not. It's real, and it's spreading."

Reznor felt her stomach drop, her mind racing. "Spreading?" she echoed. "What do you mean, spreading? Is this why I've been having these dreams? Why I feel... connected to you?"

Nocturne nodded slowly, her eyes glistening with unshed tears. "The curse binds those who come close to me. It's not just my burden anymore—it's yours, too. I tried to keep my distance, to protect you and Hamoudi, but... it's too late. You're already part of this."

Reznor's legs felt weak, and she sank to the floor across from Nocturne, her gaze locked on her friend's. "So what do we do? How do we stop it?"

Nocturne hesitated, her hands gripping the edges of the book as if it were her lifeline. "There's a ritual," she said finally, her voice barely audible. "It's dangerous, but it might be the only way to break the curse. If it works, we could end this—end centuries of suffering. But if it fails..."

Her words trailed off, and the silence that followed was deafening. Reznor reached out, covering Nocturne's trembling hand with her own. "You don't have to do this alone," she said, her voice steady despite the storm of emotions raging inside her. "Whatever this is, we'll face it together. I promise."

Nocturne's lips trembled as a faint smile crossed her face, a flicker of hope breaking through the shadows in her eyes. "Thank you," she whispered, her voice cracking.

At that moment, the sound of heavy footsteps echoed in the hallway outside, followed by a sharp knock on the door. Both women turned toward the noise, their hearts pounding. Nocturne rose to her feet, hesitating before opening the door to reveal Hamoudi, his face etched with concern.

"Okay, what the hell is going on?" Hamoudi demanded, stepping inside without waiting for an invitation. "Reznor called me earlier, and now you've both gone radio silent? If this is some kind of secret meeting, I'm offended I wasn't invited."

Reznor exchanged a glance with Nocturne before standing and facing him. "It's not... exactly that," she said, her voice uncertain. "Hamoudi, there's something you need to know."

Hamoudi's eyes narrowed as he looked between them. "I'm listening."

Reznor took a deep breath and explained everything—the dreams, the curse, the ritual. She spoke quickly, the words tumbling out as she tried to make him understand the gravity of the situation. Hamoudi's expression shifted from confusion to disbelief to something resembling reluctant acceptance.

"So, let me get this straight," he said finally, crossing his arms. "There's a centuries-old curse, it's somehow tied to Nocturne's family, and now we're all involved because we're close to her. And the only way to break it is to do some dangerous, ancient ritual?"

"That's the gist of it," Nocturne said quietly.

Hamoudi sighed, rubbing a hand over his face. "You know, I was hoping for a quiet night of binge-watching bad TV, but sure, why not? Let's break a curse."

Reznor couldn't help but smile at his dry humor, the tension in the room easing slightly. "You're in?" she asked.

"Of course I'm in," Hamoudi said, his tone softening. "You two are my best friends. I'm not letting you go through this alone."

Nocturne's eyes filled with gratitude as she looked at him. "Thank you," she said, her voice trembling.

Hamoudi clapped his hands together, his expression determined. "So, when do we start this ritual?"

Nocturne glanced at the book in her hands, her grip tightening. "Soon," she said firmly. "We do it when we are ready because I can't take any chances."

And with that, the three of them sat together, preparing to face the unknown—bound not just by the curse, but by an unbreakable bond of friendship and trust.

CHAPTER FIVE

THE RITUAL

The Delacroix attic was a graveyard of forgotten lives. Dusty trunks, yellowed letters, and fractured mementos of a family haunted by tragedy cluttered the space. Nocturne had always avoided it—there was something suffocating about being surrounded by the remnants of people who had carried the curse before her. But one restless afternoon, compelled by an inexplicable pull, she found herself standing in the attic's dim light, staring at an old trunk with a rusted lock.

It opened with surprising ease, and there, nestled under a pile of moth-eaten fabric, was a journal. Marguerite's name was inscribed on the leather cover in a delicate, almost trembling hand.

When Nocturne flipped through its pages for the first time, it felt like Marguerite's voice was whispering directly to her. The entries were a window into a life consumed by desperation, each page heavy with the sorrow of a mother who would sacrifice anything for her child. She described the pact she made, the ancient being she summoned, and the curse that tethered itself to her bloodline. Every generation would pay a price, and every descendant would carry a piece of that darkness. She felt her life crumbling in front of her as she allowed each word to register in her mind not understanding that she had friends who would willingly give up their lives to save her.

A week later, Nocturne sat in her room with Reznor and Hamoudi, the journal laid open between them. The atmosphere was tense, the gravity of what she was about to share weighing heavily on her.

"My family's cursed," Nocturne said finally, breaking the silence.

Reznor furrowed her brow, exchanging a glance with Hamoudi. "Cursed how?"

Nocturne took a deep breath, running her fingers along the journal's edges. "In the 18th century, my ancestor, Marguerite Delacroix, made a pact with...something. Her son, Philippe, was dying of some unknown illness. Medicine couldn't save him, so she turned to black magic. She summoned an entity—something ancient and cruel. In exchange for Philippe's life, she offered herself, her bloodline. But the entity twisted the deal. Philippe lived, but the Delacroix family became bound to the curse."

Hamoudi's normally cheerful face turned serious. "What does the curse actually do?"

"It feeds on us," Nocturne said, her voice trembling. "Our happiness, our futures. Every Delacroix ends up consumed by misfortune—accidents, madness, death. It's always there, lurking in the shadows, waiting for the right moment to strike."

Reznor leaned forward, her expression unreadable. "And you think this ritual can stop it?"

Nocturne nodded. "It's our only chance. Marguerite wrote about it—she believed it could sever the bond between the curse and her bloodline. But it requires sacrifice. Not just mine—yours, too."

Hamoudi placed a reassuring hand on her shoulder. "We're with you, Nocturne. Whatever it takes."

Reznor nodded in agreement. "We've come this far. We're not backing out now."

The weeks leading up to the ritual were a blur of preparation, tension, and whispered fears. The three of them—Nocturne, Reznor, and Hamoudi—found themselves entangled in a web of determination and dread, knowing that what lay ahead could change their lives forever. Marguerite's journal had been their guide, its ancient pages detailing the ritual needed to confront the

Delacroix curse. Every word felt heavy, carrying centuries of pain and desperation.

The journal spoke of a pact sealed in blood and bound by shadows. It described the curse as a living entity, a dark force that fed on the Delacroix bloodline, growing stronger with every generation. Marguerite's desperate attempt to save her son had tethered the curse to her descendants, binding them to a cycle of suffering. But there was hope—a ritual that could sever the bond, provided the vessel, Nocturne, had the strength to confront it head-on.

The preparation required precision. Over two weeks, they scoured the city for rare and symbolic items. Reznor discovered a jeweler who reluctantly parted with a piece of pure silver, while Hamoudi braved the eerie quiet of a cemetery to collect moonlit water from an ancient well. Nocturne herself contributed the final piece: locks of hair from all three of them, representing their unity and shared resolve.

As they gathered the components, their bond deepened. Nights were spent in Nocturne's dimly lit room, pouring over the journal and practicing the incantation. Hamoudi, ever the optimist, broke the tension with jokes that earned reluctant smiles, while Reznor brought a steady, calming presence. And Nocturne—Nocturne carried the weight of their shared mission, her shoulders heavy with the knowledge that her fate would determine theirs.

The night of the ritual arrived beneath the glow of a full moon. They had chosen the Delacroix Forest, the site of Marguerite's original pact. It was said to be a place where the veil between realms was thin, where the shadows were alive. The forest was deathly silent as they stepped into the clearing, the ancient trees looming overhead like silent sentinels.

The forest clearing stood still, as if it had been waiting for them for centuries. The towering oaks, gnarled and ancient, loomed like silent sentinels, their branches intertwining to create a natural cathedral. The ground was carpeted with damp moss and scattered leaves, the earthy scent mingling with the sharp tang of fear in the air.

Nocturne, Reznor, and Hamoudi moved methodically, each step deliberate, each breath steady—though beneath the surface, their hearts raced like caged birds. This wasn't just a ritual; it was a gamble with forces older and darker than anything they had encountered.

Hamoudi crouched at the edge of the clearing, the white chalk in his hand trembling ever so slightly as he etched the ritual circle into the earth. Each line was painstakingly precise, every rune copied directly from Marguerite Delacroix's journal. The symbols glinted faintly under the moonlight, a strange iridescence emanating from the chalk as though the runes themselves recognized the gravity of what was about to unfold.

Reznor, ever meticulous, placed the candles in a perfect ring around the circle. The flames sprang to life with each strike of her match, their golden glow illuminating the runes and casting elongated shadows that flickered and danced across the clearing. Her hands were steady, but her heart thudded in her chest. Every flicker of the flames felt like a pulse, as though the clearing itself had a heartbeat.

At the center of it all stood Nocturne, clutching Marguerite's journal as if it were a shield. Her dark hair framed her face, her expression one of grim determination. She stared at the pages, the faded ink almost indecipherable, but she had studied the words enough to recite them by heart. Each syllable was a thread in the tapestry of a curse that had ensnared her family for generations—a curse she was determined to unravel tonight.

"This is it," Nocturne whispered, her voice barely audible over the sound of the wind rustling through the trees.

Reznor stepped closer, her hand briefly brushing Nocturne's shoulder. "You're not alone," she said softly, her voice steady despite the fear lurking in her eyes.

Hamoudi, having completed the circle, stood and wiped his hands on his jeans, leaving faint smudges of chalk. "We've got this," he said, his characteristic optimism faltering only slightly.

"Whatever happens, we're in this together."

Nocturne nodded, her grip tightening on the journal. "Once I start, there's no turning back."

The chant began softly, a low, melodic murmur that seemed to blend with the natural sounds of the forest. The words flowed from Nocturne's lips, ancient and rhythmic, a language older than time itself. Each syllable resonated in the still night air, carrying a weight that pressed down on their chests.

The runes etched into the earth began to glow faintly, a soft, eerie light that pulsed in time with the cadence of Nocturne's voice. The candles flickered, their flames elongating unnaturally as if reaching for something unseen. The air grew colder, a biting chill that seeped into their bones.

As the chant continued, the silver piece in the center of the circle began to tremble. Its surface rippled like liquid, though it remained solid, its glow intensifying with every word. Beside it, the vial of moonlit water quivered before shattering without warning. The liquid seeped into the ground, and a faint, otherworldly glow began to spread outward from the center of the circle, illuminating the runes with an almost sinister brilliance.

The shadows at the edge of the clearing began to move. At first, it was subtle—a flicker here, a ripple there. But soon, the darkness seemed to come alive, slithering and twisting like serpents. The trees groaned, their ancient limbs creaking as if recoiling from the encroaching malevolence.

Hamoudi and Reznor exchanged a glance, their fear mirrored in each other's eyes. The pull in their chests began—a deep, unsettling sensation, as though invisible threads were being unraveled from their very souls. Reznor clutched her chest, her breathing shallow. Hamoudi gritted his teeth, his fists clenched at his sides.

"Nocturne..." Reznor's voice was barely a whisper, trembling with both fear and urgency.

Nocturne didn't falter. Her chant grew louder, more forceful, her voice cutting through the growing cacophony. The shadows converged, swirling into a vortex above the circle. Faces began to emerge within the darkness—twisted, anguished visages that contorted in silent screams. These were the spirits of the Delacroix ancestors, their pain and torment woven into the fabric of the curse. Their hollow eyes bore into Nocturne, accusing, pleading, despairing.

Tears streamed down Nocturne's face as she confronted the darkness. It wasn't just a curse—it was a living memory, a collective agony passed down through generations. She saw Marguerite Delacroix, her face etched with sorrow as she sealed the pact that had doomed her bloodline. She saw Philippe, alive but hollow, his life bought at the expense of countless others.

The shadows within the vortex began to coalesce, taking on a more defined form. A towering figure emerged, its body a swirling mass of darkness and decay. Its eyes burned with an unnatural light, piercing and unrelenting. This was the heart of the curse, the entity Marguerite had summoned centuries ago—a being of pure malevolence.

The entity's voice echoed through the clearing, a guttural, otherworldly growl that resonated in their very bones. "You dare to defy me?" it snarled, its tone a mixture of rage and amusement. "You, a mere child of the Delacroix line, think you can break the chains of fate?"

Nocturne's voice wavered but did not break. "By the blood of the past, I sever this bond! By the will of the present, I banish this curse!"

The entity laughed, a sound that sent shivers down their spines. "You cannot banish what you do not understand. This curse is as much a part of you as the blood in your veins."

The pull in their chests became unbearable, the pain searing and unrelenting. Hamoudi fell to his knees, gasping for air, while Reznor clung to the edge of the circle, her knuckles white. But they did not break. They held on, grounding each other as Nocturne stood firm against the entity's onslaught.

The vortex above them roared, the faces of the ancestors screaming silently as they were drawn into the light. Nocturne's chant reached a crescendo, her voice breaking with raw emotion. She held the journal high, its pages glowing with an ethereal light.

"With this final act, I free my bloodline!" she cried.

The entity lunged toward her, its clawed hands reaching for her, but it was too late. The silver piece in the circle exploded in a burst of light, the force knocking them all to the ground. The entity let out a deafening roar as it was pulled into the vortex, its form disintegrating into the night.

When the light faded, the clearing was silent. The shadows were gone, the runes smudged and lifeless. The candles had burned down to stubs, their smoke curling into the cold night air.

Reznor and Hamoudi looked over at Nocturne, only to see her lay motionless at the center of the circle. Reznor and Hamoudi crawled to her side, their faces pale and streaked with tears.

"Is it over?" Hamoudi asked, his voice barely above a whisper.

Nocturne opened her eyes, her gaze unfocused but filled with an overwhelming sense of relief. "I think...it's finally over," she murmured.

The weight of centuries had lifted, leaving behind an emptiness that would take time to fill. The scars of the curse would linger, but for the first time, Nocturne felt a fragile flicker of hope.

Reznor wrapped an arm around her, pulling her close. "We did it," she whispered, her voice choked with emotion.

As they sat together in the clearing, the first rays of dawn broke through the trees, casting a soft, golden light over the scene. The Delacroix curse was a shadow of the past, but their bond was the light that would guide them forward.

Whatever lay ahead, they would face it together.

CHAPTER SIX

A Rift in the Shadows

The days following the ritual were a strange limbo of relief and unease. Nocturne was undeniably different—lighter, somehow, as if an invisible yoke had been lifted from her shoulders. Her once-guarded demeanor began to crack, revealing glimpses of the person she might have been all along, unburdened by the Delacroix curse. She smiled more often now, her laughter like a melody none of them had heard before. It was tentative at first, as if she didn't quite trust the joy bubbling up from within her, but it was there, and it was real.

Reznor noticed these changes with a bittersweet pride. They had done it—or so she told herself. They had faced the abyss and come out the other side. Yet, beneath Nocturne's newfound vibrancy, there lingered an uneasiness that none of them could fully articulate. The shadows of what they had confronted refused to dissipate entirely, and the cost of their victory hung in the air like smoke.

Hamoudi, for one, was not the same. The spark in his dark eyes—the mischievous, quick-witted energy that had always defined him—had dimmed. He wasn't cracking jokes anymore, not even the sarcastic jabs that used to keep Reznor and Nocturne rolling their eyes. Instead, his silences spoke louder than words, and his smiles, when they came, were strained. Reznor noticed the change immediately, and as the days dragged on, it gnawed at her.

She finally decided to confront him a week after the ritual. It was a gray afternoon, the sky heavy with unshed rain. Reznor caught up to Hamoudi as they left school, her boots crunching against the damp gravel.

"Hamoudi, wait," she called out.

He stopped but didn't turn, his posture stiff, his hands shoved deep into the pockets of his jacket.

"Walk with me," she said, stepping beside him.

They wandered toward a nearby park, their footsteps the only sound between them. When they reached a secluded bench under a sprawling oak tree, Reznor sat down, patting the spot beside her. Hamoudi hesitated but eventually joined her, his gaze fixed on the ground.

"You've been different," she said softly, cutting straight to the point.

He let out a humorless chuckle. "Different how?"

"Quiet. Distant. It's not like you."

Hamoudi ran a hand through his hair, his jaw tight. "I'm fine, Rez. Don't worry about it."

But she did worry. She could see it in the way his shoulders sagged, in the way his fingers twitched like they wanted to fidget but couldn't find the energy.

"Talk to me," she urged. "I know that ritual was...a lot. It was for all of us. But you don't have to go through it alone."

For a moment, Hamoudi didn't respond. Then, with a deep sigh, he looked at her, and the raw vulnerability in his eyes took her breath away.

"I keep thinking," he said, his voice low, "what if we didn't do it right? What if we missed something, or worse, messed something up? Rez, I can't shake this feeling that...we didn't win. Not completely."

Reznor's chest tightened. She wanted to tell him he was wrong, that everything was fine, that they had done what they set out to do. But the words caught in her throat because, deep down, she wasn't sure.

"We were careful," she said instead, her voice steadier than she felt. "We followed the journal to the letter. We did everything we could."

"Did we?" Hamoudi challenged, his gaze piercing. "Because I keep seeing it, Rez. The shadows. I feel them, even now. Like they're watching us, waiting for something."

Reznor had no answer for that.

The unease only grew in the weeks that followed. Little things, at first—small, inexplicable occurrences that were easy to dismiss as coincidence.

One day, while walking with Nocturne through the school hallway, they passed by a glass trophy case. The instant they were beside it, the glass shattered with an earsplitting crash, shards scattering across the floor. No one was hurt, but the timing was too perfect, the air too charged.

Another time, the three of them were at Nocturne's house, curled up in her living room for a movie night. The lights flickered once, twice, and then plunged them into darkness. When they came back on a few minutes later, the room felt colder, the shadows deeper.

Reznor tried to brush these moments off—bad wiring, bad luck—but the incidents piled up like stones on her chest, and with each one, Hamoudi grew more withdrawn.

It was during one of these movie nights, a storm rumbling in the distance, that Hamoudi finally voiced what had been weighing on all of them. The movie credits were rolling, the room illuminated by the bluish glow of the TV screen.

"Nocturne," Hamoudi said abruptly, his tone serious.

She looked up from where she sat cross-legged on the floor, the bowl of popcorn forgotten in her lap.

"Do you feel...different since the ritual?"

Reznor stiffened, shooting him a warning look. "Hamoudi, don't—"

"It's okay," Nocturne interrupted, her gaze dropping to the carpet. She took a deep breath before answering.

"Sometimes," she admitted. "Most days, I feel...free. Like the curse is really gone. But other times..." She trailed off, her voice trembling.

"Other times, what?" Hamoudi pressed, his voice deeper now.

Nocturne hesitated, her hands twisting in her lap. "Sometimes it feels like...like there's something still lingering. A shadow I can't shake."

Reznor's heart sank. "Why didn't you tell us?"

Nocturne looked up, guilt and fear etched into her features. "Because I didn't want to worry you. You both gave so much for me, risked so much. I didn't want you to think it was all for nothing."

"It wasn't for nothing," Reznor said firmly, sliding off the couch to sit beside her. She placed a hand on Nocturne's arm. "We did this to help you, and we're not stopping now. If something's wrong, we'll fix it. Together."

Hamoudi nodded, his expression softening for the first time in weeks. "She's right. You're not alone in this. You never were."

Nocturne's lips curved into a faint, watery smile. "Thank you. Both of you."

They sat there in silence for a while, the storm outside growing louder. The shadows in the room seemed to stretch and shift with each flash of lightning, their edges too sharp, too alive.

Reznor tried to ignore the feeling creeping up her spine, the sense that something was watching them from just beyond the circle of light.

And as the storm raged on, the shadows lingered, silent and waiting.

Despite their words of reassurance and promises of unity, an invisible tension coiled tighter between the three of them, a silent undercurrent that none dared to name. Hamoudi's gnawing doubts, Nocturne's fragile composure, and Reznor's desperate need to hold them together wove an intricate web of unease. It was as if they were orbiting a shared truth too heavy to confront, their closeness paradoxically pulling them apart.

The breaking point came on a cold Friday night at Obsidian Veil, the underground club where the trio often sought solace. The venue was alive with hedonistic energy, a pulse of smoke, leather, and electricity that vibrated in their chests. Shadows and neon lights danced together on sweat-slicked walls, and the relentless bass of industrial beats thudded like a war drum.

For the first time in weeks, it felt like things might be okay. The three of them let themselves dissolve into the crowd, their bodies moving to the music like they were trying to escape their own shadows. Nocturne laughed when Hamoudi's awkward dancing earned him an exaggerated spin from a stranger. Reznor spun her friend in retaliation, their shared laughter bright enough to cut through the darkness.

For a fleeting moment, they were just three friends again—no curses, no rituals, no lingering fears.

But peace never lingered long for them.

The illusion shattered at the bar.

As they approached, weaving through a maze of bodies, a man stumbled into Nocturne, spilling his drink down the front of her black dress.

"Shit—sorry about that," he said hastily, his voice drowned out by the music.

Nocturne opened her mouth to respond, but before she could, there was a sharp creak overhead. A split second later, a light fixture broke free from the ceiling and crashed down, narrowly missing the man's head.

The entire bar seemed to inhale at once.

The man stumbled backward, his face pale and twisted with shock. "What the hell just happened?"

"I...I don't know," Nocturne stammered, her voice trembling.

The man's gaze darkened, his lips curling into a sneer. "You're bad luck, lady."

"Hey, watch your mouth," Hamoudi snapped, stepping forward to shield Nocturne. His voice carried an edge of warning that cut through the tension.

The man muttered something under his breath and stalked away, but the damage was done. The weight of his accusation lingered like cigarette smoke, clinging to them as they left the club and walked to a nearby park.

The cold air bit at their skin as they sat beneath the skeletal branches of an old tree. A streetlight flickered overhead, its glow casting long, shifting shadows across the damp grass.

Hamoudi was the first to speak, his voice low and tight. "What the hell was that back there?"

"I don't know," Nocturne whispered, her arms wrapped around herself as if trying to ward off more than the cold. "I didn't do anything."

"Maybe not," Hamoudi said, pacing now. "But this kind of shit keeps happening around you, Nocturne. How do we know the curse is really gone?"

"Hamoudi, stop," Reznor said, her voice sharp and commanding.

"No, she needs to hear this!" he shot back, spinning to face her. His hands were clenched at his sides, his expression a mixture of fear and frustration. "We put everything into that ritual. Everything. And now? Now it feels like we're back where we started, except worse. How are we supposed to move on if we don't even know if it worked?"

"That's enough!" Reznor snapped, stepping between them. Her heart pounded in her chest, a mixture of anger and desperation. "This isn't helping."

Hamoudi's expression crumbled, his bravado fading as quickly as it had flared. He turned away, dragging a hand through his hair. "I'm sorry," he muttered, his voice barely audible. "I'm just...I'm scared, okay? I'm scared of losing you. Both of you."

Nocturne's eyes softened, the shadows of guilt and doubt that had clouded her face giving way to something more fragile. She reached out, placing a hand on his arm. "You won't lose us," she said quietly, her voice trembling with sincerity. "I promise."

Reznor's chest tightened as she looked at them—her two best friends, both terrified, both trying so hard to hold onto something that felt like it was slipping away. She wanted to fix it, to say something that would erase the tension and fear that had taken root in their lives. But she didn't know how.

The next day, Reznor decided she couldn't just sit back and hope for the best anymore. If there were answers to be found, she would find them.

She spent the entire day buried in research, poring over dusty old tomes, obscure online forums, and anything else she could get her hands on. Her room was a mess of open books and scrawled notes, the faint smell of burnt coffee lingering in the air.

By the time the sun set, she felt she had a clearer picture of what they were dealing with. The curse wasn't just about bad luck—it thrived on fear and doubt, feeding off the cracks in their unity like a parasite.

That evening, she gathered Hamoudi and Nocturne in her room. The atmosphere was tense but determined.

"We've been thinking about this the wrong way," she began, pacing as she spoke. "The curse isn't just about causing bad things to happen. It's about feeding off us—off our fear, our doubts, our anger. The more we let it get to us, the stronger it becomes."

Hamoudi frowned. "So, what? We just...pretend everything's fine?"

"No," Reznor said firmly. "We face it. Together. We don't let it divide us. That's the only way to beat it."

For a moment, silence hung in the air, thick and heavy. Then Hamoudi nodded. "I'm in."

Nocturne looked between them, her expression softening as a faint smile tugged at her lips. "Me too."

Reznor reached out, clasping both of their hands tightly in hers. "We've faced the darkness before, and we're still standing. Whatever comes next, we face it together. No more fear, no more doubt. Just us."

As their hands remained clasped, a quiet strength filled the room. The shadows seemed to retreat, if only for a moment, and for the first time in weeks, Reznor felt the faint flicker of hope.

They had come this far, and they wouldn't let the darkness win. Not now. Not ever.

CHAPTER SEVEN

FRACTURES AND FORTITUDE

The uneasy truce between Nocturne, Reznor, and Hamoudi held for the next week, but its fragility became increasingly impossible to ignore. The more they pretended everything was fine, the more the tension seemed to creep into every interaction, a constant undertone that hummed beneath their surface attempts at normalcy. It was as if the very act of trying to heal had become a wound in itself, growing deeper with every passing day.

The events at Obsidian Veil, the light fixture falling, the angry words from that stranger—they weighed on them all, though none of them spoke about it aloud. Each time one of them brushed against the subject, the air seemed to thicken, like the room was full of smoke they couldn't escape. There was something wrong, and though none of them could place it exactly, it was there, gnawing at the edges of their minds.

Reznor tried desperately to be the glue that would hold them together. She suggested late-night study sessions, offered up distractions like spontaneous outings to their favorite diners, and even threw out the idea of a group project for school—something that could keep their minds busy and their hearts in sync. But no matter how many diversions she introduced, the distance between them grew. The lighthearted moments felt like brief respites before the storm, and it only made the tension more unbearable when the laughter subsided.

By the time Wednesday evening arrived, the strain had become unbearable, a pressure in the air that none of them could shake. It had been raining heavily for hours, a relentless downpour that mirrored the unease swirling between them. Reznor had hoped that tonight, a quiet night spent at Nocturne's house, might break the spell. She arrived first, drenched from head to toe, the rainwater soaking her jacket and leaving her skin chilled. As she walked through the door, she found Nocturne in the living room, sitting on the floor amidst a chaos of books and candles, her eyes red and tired, her expression distant.

"You've been at it again?" Reznor asked, her voice strained but gentle as she set a bag of snacks on the coffee table and shook the water from her coat.

Nocturne barely looked up, her voice soft and strained, like she was exhausted from carrying a weight too heavy for her small frame. "I just wanted to double-check something. About the curse."

Reznor sighed, pushing her wet hair from her face as she knelt beside her. "We've been through this, Nocturne. The ritual worked. You're free. It's over."

"Then why does it still feel like something's wrong?" Nocturne's voice quivered, and there was a tremor in her hands as she brushed a strand of dark hair from her face. "Why do these things keep happening? The accidents. The shadows. It's like the curse is still... here."

Reznor froze. The words, though familiar, were beginning to sound like an echo of something she didn't want to hear. She wanted to reassure Nocturne, to wrap her in certainty and banish the doubts that clouded her mind, but the truth was, Reznor didn't have the answers. And that fact gnawed at her like an itch she couldn't scratch.

Before she could respond, the door slammed open, and Hamoudi stormed in, his boots heavy on the floor, his face flushed with frustration. The stormy look in his eyes made Reznor's stomach drop.

"You're still obsessing over that damn book?" he snapped, his tone sharp as he waved toward the mess of pages and open books surrounding Nocturne.

Reznor shot him a warning glance, but Hamoudi ignored it, his anger now an uncontrolled flame. "Enough, Reznor. We've been over this. We've all tried to move on, but she—" He gestured toward Nocturne, his voice rising, his hands trembling with the weight of his frustration, "—she keeps dragging us back into this curse nonsense!"

"It's not nonsense," Nocturne's voice was calm but firm, her eyes lifting to meet his with a cold intensity. She held herself together despite the aching vulnerability that pulsed just beneath the surface. "You've seen it, Hamoudi. The things that happen around me. It's not in my head."

Hamoudi's breath hitched, his fists clenching at his sides, as though the words were too much to bear. "Yeah, I've seen it," he said, his tone now dark with doubt. "But maybe it's not the curse. Maybe it's just—" He faltered, his throat tightening.

"Just what?" Nocturne demanded, standing up so quickly that the books around her scattered across the floor. Her eyes, wide and hurt, met his head-on, desperate for answers she wasn't sure she could hear.

"Just you," Hamoudi finished, his voice cracking under the weight of the admission. The words hung in the air like an accusation, sharp and final, and the room fell into a suffocating silence.

Nocturne froze, her body going rigid as if she had been physically struck. The world seemed to stop moving for a heartbeat, the sound of the rain outside pounding louder than the silence that stretched between them.

"You think this is my fault?" Her voice was barely above a whisper, each word laced with disbelief and hurt.

Hamoudi's shoulders slumped as though the weight of his own words had shattered him. He shook his head, the anger now replaced by something deeper, a tiredness that went beyond the frustration he had let out moments before. "I don't know what to think anymore," he confessed, his voice softer now, tinged with regret. "I just know that I can't keep living like this. Waiting for something else to go wrong. It's exhausting, and I don't know how much more I can take."

Nocturne's breath caught, the finality of his words sinking deep into her chest. Her throat tightened, and for a moment, she didn't know whether to scream or cry. She had wanted to believe that the curse was gone, that the ritual had worked, but now—now she was unsure of everything. Everything except the ache in her heart as she watched Hamoudi crumble in front of her.

Reznor stepped between them, her heart hammering in her chest. Her voice was sharp and desperate, cutting through the raw tension. "Stop it, both of you!" She didn't care if her words were too harsh. They needed to stop. They needed to hold on to something before everything fell apart. "This isn't helping."

Hamoudi stared at her, a mixture of guilt and defeat written all over his face. "I can't do this right now," he muttered, turning away from both of them. His feet moved toward the door without hesitation, his body a quiet rebellion against the vulnerability he had just exposed.

Without another word, he walked out into the storm, leaving Nocturne and Reznor standing in the heart of the silence, a distance between them that felt miles wide. The door slammed behind him, leaving nothing but the heavy sound of rain against the windows.

Reznor stood still, her mind racing, her chest tight. She wanted to say something, anything, but the words felt like they would only make things worse. So she simply turned to Nocturne, whose expression was unreadable, her body rigid with the kind of quiet devastation that spoke volumes. Reznor wanted to reach out, to hold her, but for the first time in a long while, the three of them were fractured beyond repair.

It had never been just about a curse. It had always been about the fear that lived inside them all. And now, in the wake of Hamoudi's words, Reznor realized just how deep that fear went.

That night, Reznor couldn't find rest. She lay in bed, staring up at the ceiling, her mind racing. The steady rhythm of the rain tapping against her window seemed to echo the storm inside her. Hamoudi's words kept repeating over and over, like a broken record, each one stabbing deeper into her chest. "Just you." The words reverberated in her thoughts, and for the first time in months, she questioned everything she thought she knew.

Was it Nocturne? Or was it the curse that still lingered, pulling at the threads of their bond, unraveling everything they had worked so hard to heal?

The thought made Reznor's stomach churn. How could she even entertain the idea? Nocturne was more than just her friend; she was the sister Reznor never had. They had fought tooth and nail to break the curse that had haunted Nocturne's life, and now... now it felt like they were on the verge of losing everything they'd worked for. Could the darkness that had plagued Nocturne's life truly be gone? Or was it still lurking, waiting to consume them all?

A surge of frustration shot through her. She needed answers.

Slipping out of bed, Reznor grabbed her laptop, the cool glow of the screen offering her a small comfort in the dark. For hours, she scoured obscure forums and dusty websites, reading about curses, rituals, and the supernatural. Most of it was useless—tangled webs of superstition and half-baked theories—but one post caught her eye.

A user claimed to have experience with breaking generational curses, describing how, even after a curse was lifted, its energy could linger, feeding on the fear and doubt left in its wake. The post suggested that the real solution wasn't another ritual, but something more visceral: a confrontation. A symbolic act to reclaim power over the lingering darkness.

Reznor's breath caught in her throat. The answer was so simple, so raw, that it struck her like a bolt of lightning. Could it really be this easy? Could the key to ending this curse once and for all be as simple as facing it head-on?

Determined to find out, Reznor spent the rest of the night piecing together the vague instructions from the post, her mind buzzing with adrenaline. This could work. She knew it could.

The next morning, Reznor couldn't wait to tell Nocturne what she had found. The rain had stopped, but the heavy atmosphere hung in the air, like the world was holding its breath.

She found Nocturne in the kitchen, her face pale and drawn. The exhaustion of the past week still clung to her, but when Reznor told her about the confrontation, Nocturne's eyes flickered with a mixture of skepticism and hope.

"A confrontation?" Nocturne repeated, her voice filled with uncertainty. "What does that even mean?"

"I'm not entirely sure," Reznor admitted, the weight of her own doubts still pressing against her chest. "But I think it means we need to face whatever's left of the curse. Together."

Nocturne was silent for a long moment, as though weighing Reznor's words against everything she had been through. Then, finally, she nodded slowly. "And what about Hamoudi? Do you think he'll go along with this?"

Reznor's jaw tightened. "He will," she said firmly. "I'll make sure of it."

It wasn't easy, but after a tense discussion, Hamoudi reluctantly agreed. The animosity between him and Nocturne was still there, thick as smoke, but Reznor pushed forward. She couldn't let them keep unraveling. They needed to heal. They had to heal.

The trio decided to return to the forest where they had performed the original ritual, the place where they had first fought for Nocturne's freedom. It felt fitting, like returning to the heart of it all. A final confrontation to end it, once and for all.

As the sun dipped below the horizon, casting long, eerie shadows across the trees, they arrived at the clearing. The air felt heavy, saturated with the weight of everything they had endured. Reznor could feel it—like a presence, waiting, watching.

"Are we ready?" she asked, her voice barely above a whisper, though the question was more of a challenge to herself than to either of her companions.

"As ready as we'll ever be," Hamoudi replied, his tone begrudging but tinged with something close to resolve. He wasn't sure of this, not at all, but something in his gut told him they had no other choice.

Nocturne's eyes were distant as she gazed at the place where they had once stood together, fighting to save her. Her gaze hardened, determination flickering behind the shadows of doubt. "Let's do this."

They set up the circle in the same spot, the candles trembling as they were lit, their flames dancing erratically in the wind. The supplies they had gathered—matches, incense, and the ritual book—lay before them, but this time, there was no script to follow. There was only their raw instincts, their shared bond, and the darkness that threatened to consume them.

Reznor stepped into the center of the circle, her heart pounding in her chest, her palms slick with sweat. She looked at Nocturne and Hamoudi, who stood on either side of her, their faces shadowed but resolute.

"We're here to take back what's ours," Reznor said, her voice steady, but deep down, her pulse hammered in her ears. She could feel the weight of the words pressing against her, but she stood firm. This was the only way. They had to take back their power.

Nocturne and Hamoudi joined her, forming a triangle within the circle. The shadows around them shifted, twisting like they were alive, their movement jagged and unnatural. The air grew thick, a suffocating presence surrounding them. It felt like the forest itself was holding its breath, waiting for what would come next.

"We're not afraid of you," Nocturne said, her voice strong and unwavering, though her eyes betrayed the fear that lurked beneath.

"You don't have power over us anymore," Hamoudi added, his tone just as firm, though there was an edge of desperation in his voice.

The darkness in the air seemed to grow heavier, the shadows stretching and coiling like serpents. Reznor felt a cold chill crawl down her spine, but she refused to let it break her resolve.

"We are stronger than you," Reznor declared, her voice rising above the growing cacophony of whispers and shadows. "And we're not leaving until you're gone."

The shadows shifted violently, their forms flickering and twisting, until they coalesced into a figure—a dark, shifting mass that loomed over them, its presence suffocating. The air felt thick with malice, but Reznor stood her ground. This wasn't just about Nocturne anymore. It was about all of them. It was about claiming back their lives.

"Leave her alone," Reznor shouted, her voice breaking through the growing storm of darkness. "Leave us alone!"

The figure hissed in response, its form writhing like it was in pain, like it didn't want to be banished. It didn't want to let go.

Nocturne stepped forward, her eyes blazing with a fierce fire. She had faced the curse for so long. She had let it control her for far too long. Now it was time to take back what was hers.

"You don't control me anymore," she said, her voice a sharp edge cutting through the night. "I control you."

The figure shrieked, a high-pitched wail that seemed to shake the very earth beneath their feet. And then, with one last, violent movement, the shadow dissolved into smoke, swirling in a violent whirlwind before dissipating into nothingness.

The candles flickered wildly, their flames dancing and guttering in the wind before they snuffed out completely, plunging them into darkness. For a moment, everything was still. Silent.

Then, the moon broke through the clouds, casting an ethereal glow across the clearing, illuminating them in its pale light.

"It's gone," Nocturne whispered, her voice barely audible, filled with wonder and disbelief. The weight she had carried for so long seemed to lift from her, like a fog lifting from her soul.

Reznor and Hamoudi exchanged glances, their faces breaking into smiles, relief flooding their chests. It was over.

"We did it," Hamoudi said, his voice low, tinged with disbelief. It felt unreal, like the world had shifted beneath his feet and he was still catching his breath.

Reznor pulled them both into a tight hug, her heart swelling with pride, love, and something else—a deep, aching sense of victory. "We did it together."

As the trio stood in the aftermath of the ritual, a profound sense of peace settled over them. The air felt lighter, the shadows no longer threatening.

"It's over," Nocturne said, her voice filled with wonder.

Reznor smiled, relief washing over her. "Yeah. It's over."

Hamoudi let out a shaky laugh. "Remind me never to doubt you two again."

The three of them embraced, their bond stronger than ever.

For the first time in years, Nocturne felt truly free.

And as they walked out of the forest that night, the weight of the curse was gone, but the tension between them lingered. Though they had shared in the struggle and triumph, the scars of what they had just endured ran deep. They didn't know what the future held, what challenges might come their way next, or even how to face one another just yet. The silence between them wasn't empty—it was full of unspoken words and unresolved feelings. For now, all they could do was take it one step at a time, knowing that healing, like the journey itself, would take time.

CHAPTER EIGHT

FRAGMENTS OF SILENCE

The soft hum of the city outside Reznor's window barely reached her ears, swallowed by the steady, rhythmic patter of raindrops on glass. She woke slowly, her body stiff and reluctant to leave the warmth of sleep. The overcast sky beyond her curtains struggled to push through the thick layers of clouds, offering only the faintest hint of light. The storm had passed, and with it, the restlessness that had held the world captive for hours. Now, the city lay in a quiet, somber haze, drenched in rain and heavy silence.

For the first time in what felt like an eternity, Reznor felt lighter. The curse—the force that had hung over her and her friends like an unshakable cloud—was gone. It had been vanquished, driven away by their collective will, their shared power. But even as she breathed in the crisp, rain-washed air, there was a lingering heaviness inside her chest, something she couldn't quite name. It wasn't the curse anymore. It was something deeper, more insidious. The silence between her and the others had settled in like a ghost, haunting every corner of her thoughts, and she couldn't escape it.

She let her eyes fall shut again for a moment, her thoughts tumbling over one another in a rush. There had been victory, yes. But the kind of victory that tasted bittersweet, like wine that had gone sour too quickly, leaving a dry, empty aftertaste. The curse was gone, but what had they really won? The emotional wreckage left in its wake, the fractures in their relationships—it was impossible to ignore. She could feel the weight of it pressing down on her, just as heavy as the darkness had ever been, though this time it wasn't supernatural. This time, it was human. And that made it all the harder to deal with.

Reznor's chest tightened as she thought about the others, the gulf that had widened between them. The night before had shattered something—something unspoken but so palpable in the tension that had simmered just beneath the surface. She had been there when the walls between Nocturne and Hamoudi had finally cracked open, when the anger and fear had bled out in a messy explosion of words. Her hands still trembled at the memory.

What have I done?

She had tried so hard to hold the group together, to keep the balance even when everything seemed destined to fall apart. But had she failed? Had her efforts to be the glue that held them all in place, to convince them they could overcome the darkness, only served to push them further away from each other? She had always been the one to calm the storms, to bring them back to some semblance of unity after every fight. But this time, there was no coming back from it. The rift between them had grown too wide.

The silence between Nocturne and Hamoudi felt like a chasm she couldn't bridge. Reznor hadn't been able to stop Hamoudi from storming out, hadn't been able to do anything as the words, so sharp and biting, flew between them. "Just you."

Her heart twisted at the memory. Just you—the accusation that Nocturne was somehow to blame for everything, that she had caused the chaos, that she was the reason their world had been turned upside down. Reznor had watched as Hamoudi's frustration, his fear, had bubbled over, spilling into something more toxic than any of them had anticipated. And Nocturne—Nocturne, who had been carrying the weight of that curse for so long, had stood there, stunned, silent, her pride shattered. The look on her face would haunt Reznor for days to come. It had been a crack in the foundation of their friendship, one that felt impossible to repair.

Hamoudi's guilt was palpable, festering in the space between them. His words had been a defense mechanism, a reaction to the overwhelming fear that gripped him. But Reznor had seen the guilt gnawing at him, could feel the strain of it in every tense silence, in every attempt to avoid eye contact. It was a burden he couldn't carry alone, but he didn't seem ready to reach out. And Nocturne—Nocturne was somewhere inside herself, somewhere deep in the silence, and Reznor didn't know how to reach her anymore.

Her fingers tightened around the phone in her hand. She stared at the screen, the words of her messages blinking back at her, both a plea and an attempt at control.

The message to Nocturne was simple: "*We need to talk. I can't do this alone. Please.*" Reznor paused, unsure of how to continue, but she couldn't hesitate any longer. She hit send.

Then, she turned her attention to Hamoudi. He had to know that this silence—this distance—was eating away at all of them. But what could she say to him that would make him understand? "*I can't fix this alone. Please don't shut me out.*"

Her thumb hovered over the keyboard for a moment, and she almost erased the message, second-guessing herself. But this wasn't the time for doubt. It wasn't the time to back down. She hit send before she could talk herself out of it.

The waiting felt endless. Her heart thudded loudly in her chest, every minute stretching into an eternity. She didn't know if either of them would respond, didn't know if her words would make any difference at all. What if they didn't care? What if they were too far gone, too wrapped up in their own grief and guilt to ever find their way back to each other?

But she had to try. She had to do something, or they would lose each other forever.

The storm outside had passed, but the one inside her—the one inside all of them—raged on, and Reznor didn't know how to stop it. She had no answers, no simple solutions. There was no magic spell to fix what had broken, no incantation to make things right. All she had was the hope that, maybe, if they could just come together, if they could face the aftermath together, they might find a way to heal.

A message pinged on her phone.

Nocturne's reply was brief, her words clipped: "*I don't know if I'm ready to talk yet.*"

Reznor's stomach sank. She had expected it, but it still hurt. She was about to type a response when another message arrived. Hamoudi. "*I know. I'm in.*"

Reznor closed her eyes, exhaling a breath she hadn't realized she'd been holding. It wasn't everything, but it was a start. It was a crack in the wall, a glimmer of light in the darkness.

She wasn't sure what came next. There was no clear path forward. But maybe, just maybe, they could begin to heal, piece by fragile piece. It wouldn't be easy. But nothing worth fighting for ever was.

Hamoudi sat slumped on his couch, the weight of the storm still hanging in the air around him. Outside, the rain had ceased, but inside his apartment, it felt like everything was suffocating. The silence was thick, a constant reminder of what had been said, what had been broken.

The confrontation, the things he had shouted at Nocturne—it was like a wound that wouldn't heal. Every time he closed his eyes, he replayed her face, the hurt in her eyes, the disbelief as his words cut through the fragile bond they had left. It was a part of him he had hoped would stay buried, yet the guilt kept him awake, gnawing at him in the dead of the night.

He hadn't meant it, not any of it. The anger that had driven him to lash out—it wasn't hers to carry. It was his own fear, his own deep-rooted insecurities that had built up over the years, the pressure of wanting to protect her and not being able to. He had convinced himself for so long that if he could just keep her safe, if he could hold everything together, nothing bad would ever happen.

But that was a lie. They were all broken in some way, and trying to fix everyone else had only shattered him in the process.

The guilt pressed down on him like a physical weight. He had done what he always did: he acted out of fear, out of desperation. But this time, the consequences were undeniable. He had pushed Nocturne away at the moment she needed him the most. And in doing so, he had fractured the very thing they'd all worked so hard to preserve.

Hamoudi reached for his phone, his fingers brushing against the cold screen. The act of picking it up felt monumental, like it would somehow fix everything—or make it worse. He wasn't sure which. The weight of the decision to reach out to Nocturne hung heavily in the air. But could he truly fix what had been broken?

He knew what he had to do. He had to tell her the truth, even if it terrified him. He needed to apologize, to explain that it wasn't her fault. That it was his fear, his need to control everything, that had driven him to lash out. But the words stuck in his throat, and his fingers trembled as they hovered over the keys. What if she didn't want to hear it? What if it was too late?

His phone buzzed in his hand, breaking the silence. He glanced down and saw it was a message from Reznor. *"I can't fix this alone. Please don't shut me out."*

For a moment, he just stared at the words. The weight of Reznor's plea settled over him. This wasn't just about him and Nocturne anymore. It was about all of them. The trio had been shattered, and it wasn't just the curse they needed to confront—it was the emotional wreckage, the silence, the unspoken truths that had been festering between them.

Reznor was reaching out because she needed them, because she understood the importance of coming together and healing the fractures they had allowed to form. Hamoudi's chest tightened at the thought. He couldn't keep hiding, couldn't keep running from the mess they had created. It was time to face the music.

He set the phone down for a moment, closing his eyes and taking a deep breath. He had to apologize. Not just to Nocturne, but to himself too. For allowing fear to dictate his actions, for letting the anger overpower his love and loyalty to her. She deserved better than that.

With a sense of finality, he picked up the phone again. His fingers moved, slow and deliberate, as he typed a message to Nocturne.

"I'm sorry. For everything. For the things I said. I was afraid. I'm scared that I've lost you, that I've ruined everything. But I'm willing to do whatever it takes to fix this. If you'll let me."

The words felt too heavy to be true, yet they were. He had to let her know the depth of his regret, had to explain that the anger wasn't her fault, that it was his own fear, his own insecurity. He wanted to fix it, wanted to fix them.

Once the message was sent, Hamoudi stared at the screen for what felt like an eternity, his heart racing as the ticks turned blue, signaling she had opened his message. Would she reply? Would she believe him?

He wasn't sure what would happen next. The emotional distance between them had been growing for weeks, and the confrontation had only deepened the divide. But he had to try. For her. For them.

His fingers hovered over the screen again, ready to type more if she needed it, but he stopped himself. There was nothing more to say just yet. He had to wait for her response. All he could do now was hope she would give him the chance to show her that he could be better—that he could be the man she needed him to be, if she would let him.

The waiting was excruciating and Hamoudi's fingers hovered over his phone for a moment longer, his thoughts swirling in a chaotic, tangled mess. He had just sent the message to Nocturne, hoping against hope that it would be enough. But there was still the matter of Reznor—of their fragile unity as a trio. The guilt he felt for what had happened between him and Nocturne bled into the worry for what Reznor must have been feeling. She had been the one to try to hold them all together, to keep them moving forward despite everything.

He reached for his phone again, fingers trembling slightly as he scrolled to Reznor's message, the words on the screen reminding him of what was at stake. *"I can't fix this alone. Please don't shut me out."*

Hamoudi had never felt the weight of his actions more than now. He couldn't stay hidden in his own guilt and fear. Reznor was reaching out because she, too, knew that the time had come for them to confront the wreckage they'd allowed to fester. He had to respond, to show that he was willing to face it all—not just with Nocturne, but with her too.

With a deep breath, he typed his reply.

"I know. I'm in."

The words felt simple, yet they were loaded with meaning. It wasn't just an affirmation to Reznor's plea—it was a declaration to himself too. He wasn't backing down anymore. He wasn't going to hide in his own shame. Whatever came next, whatever they needed to confront, he was in. He was ready to be part of the solution, to help rebuild what had been broken, no matter how hard it might be.

Hamoudi pressed send, then leaned back against the couch, his heart racing as the dots appeared on the screen. It wasn't much—just a few words—but it was the first step toward something real. Something that could start to heal the silence that had settled over all of them.

He didn't know what the future held, but at least for the first time in a long while, he felt like he was doing something right.

Nocturne spent the day in solitude, cocooned in the silence of her apartment. The rain had stopped, but its memory lingered in the air, heavy and damp, as though the world itself was still soaked in the aftermath. The storm outside had passed, but inside, Nocturne felt like she was still drowning in it. The ritual was over. The curse had been lifted. But now that it was gone, what exactly had she gained?

She sat slouched on the couch, knees pulled tightly to her chest, the faint flicker of a candle casting eerie shadows across the room.

The dim, trembling light seemed to mock her, its warm glow barely enough to push back the oppressive weight of the darkness that hung around her. It was as though the curse itself still hovered in the corners of the room, lingering like an uninvited guest. But she knew it wasn't true. The curse had been destroyed. The ritual had worked. She was free.

And yet, she didn't feel free.

Nocturne couldn't help but trace the emptiness that had settled inside her—an imaginary vast, cavernous hole where the curse had once been, a hollow space that no longer had a purpose. For years, she had lived under its shadow, the dark weight shaping her every action, her every thought. It had been the force that kept her going, the reason she had kept her distance from everyone else. It had been her constant companion, a suffocating presence that defined her existence. And now, with it gone, she was left with nothing but the eerie quiet of her own mind.

She ran a hand through her hair, her fingers trembling as they passed over the strands, tangled and unkempt from the hours of solitude. She had fought so hard for this. She had pushed and clawed her way through the darkness, desperate to free herself. But now that it was over, she was paralyzed by the very thing she had longed for: freedom.

Who was she without the curse? Without the constant threat of darkness trailing her every step? She had never considered a life without it, never dared to imagine a future where the shadows didn't cling to her every move. Now, it felt as though she was drifting—lost, untethered. The world around her seemed so ordinary now, so normal. How was she supposed to fit into that? Could she ever truly live like everyone else, free from the weight she had carried for so long?

The silence in her apartment was unbearable. It wrapped around her like a shroud, suffocating her with its stillness. She had grown so used to the chaos, to the noise that came with the curse—the constant sense that something was always lurking just beneath the surface, waiting to break free. Now, with that constant tension gone, there was only the quiet. And it was as unsettling as it was foreign.

For the first time in her life, she felt completely alone. Not just physically, but emotionally, too. Her mind wandered back to the past few days, to the confrontation, to Hamoudi's words. The rage he had unleashed on her—accusations, blame—it still burned, still stung like an open wound. She had expected anger from him, had known it was coming, but she hadn't been prepared for how deeply it would wound her. Just you, he had said, his voice dripping with frustration. His words were a knife in her chest, and no matter how much she tried to convince herself it was just fear, just panic, it didn't change the fact that it had shattered something inside of her.

Had she really ruined everything? The guilt that had clung to her since the ritual only deepened. Her thoughts spiraled—was she the cause of this rift? Had the curse made her into someone so consumed by fear and pain that she had driven away the people who cared about her? She thought of Hamoudi, of his pain, his fear. She understood it, but the sharpness of his words, the blame he had cast on her, still left her reeling. Could things ever go back to the way they were? Could they ever rebuild what had been broken?

Her heart clenched as she thought of him. He had been her anchor, her confidant, the one person who had never judged her, who had always tried to protect her. And yet, in that moment of anger, she felt as though she had lost him. She hadn't expected him to understand the full weight of what she had gone through. She hadn't expected him to fully forgive her, but the things he said still felt like a betrayal. She had tried so hard to protect him, to protect them both, but in the end, the curse had driven a wedge between them. And now, that rift seemed impossible to cross.

Nocturne didn't know how to fix this. She didn't know if she even could. The distance between them felt too great, too wide. She could feel the gulf growing between them, the silent spaces in their conversations, the unsaid words that loomed large in the air. She wanted to reach out to him, to apologize, to explain herself. But how could she, when she didn't even know who she was anymore? She was still trying to make sense of the woman she had become, let alone the one she wanted to be.

Her phone buzzed, cutting through the fog of her thoughts. It was a message from Reznor. *"We need to talk. I can't do this alone. Please."*

Nocturne stared at the screen, her heart sinking. She didn't want to face them. Didn't want to confront the mess they had made of everything. It felt easier to stay in this cocoon of silence, to hide away from the damage they had all caused. But Reznor was right. The silence had gone on long enough. She couldn't avoid it any longer. It was time to face what had happened, time to confront the wreckage that lay between them all.

She wanted to reply. Wanted to tell Reznor that she wasn't ready, that she needed more time, that she wasn't sure if she could face them just yet. But deep down, she knew it wasn't just about her. It wasn't just about the curse or the emotional wreckage it had left behind. It was about the people she had come to care about—the people who had fought beside her, who had shared the pain, the loss, and the fear. If she didn't make the first move, if she didn't take the first step toward healing, they might all just slip away.

Nocturne inhaled deeply, staring at the message for a long moment. Then, she typed a response: *"I don't know if I'm ready to talk yet."*

It wasn't a definitive no, at least. It was just the truth, as painful as it was to admit. She wasn't sure if she could fix things, or if things could even be fixed. But maybe—just maybe—there was a sliver of hope, a small chance that if they could talk, if they could face this together, they could start to heal.

Nocturne stared at Reznor's message for a long while, her heart heavy. *We need to talk. I can't do this alone. Please.* The words echoed in her mind, urging her to confront what she had been avoiding. As much as she wanted to shut herself off, bury herself in the silence of her apartment, the truth gnawed at her. They couldn't heal if they continued to pretend nothing had happened.

She hadn't expected it—this call for openness, for some form of resolution—but Reznor was right. They couldn't keep running from the damage they had done to each other. Nocturne knew she was partially responsible for the fracture between them, but it still felt like a painful wound she wasn't ready to touch. Her fingers hovered over the screen, unsure whether she was ready to face the emotional weight that would come with it.

Just as she was about to put the phone down, it buzzed again. This time, it was a message from Hamoudi.

"I'm sorry. For everything. For the things I said. I was afraid. I'm scared that I've lost you, that I've ruined everything. But I'm willing to do whatever it takes to fix this. If you'll let me."

Her breath caught in her throat. She could hear the rawness in his words, the vulnerability that had been hidden beneath the anger he'd thrown at her the night before. It was like he was admitting to himself that he, too, didn't know how to navigate the mess they had found themselves in, but he was still reaching out. Still wanting to fight for what they once had.

Nocturne leaned back against the couch, her phone still in her hand. His message was different from Reznor's. Reznor's felt like an invitation to a deeper understanding, a plea for them to come together. Hamoudi's, on the other hand, was tentative, fragile, as if he was unsure if there was even anything left to salvage. But the honesty in it, the raw openness, made Nocturne's chest tighten.

She had hurt him. She had pushed him away, even when he needed her most. She had let the curse define her, let it control her every move, every interaction. And now, after all that, Hamoudi was offering an olive branch—one that Nocturne wasn't sure she was ready to accept, but knew she needed to.

Her thumb hovered over the keyboard, but she hesitated. She didn't want to say the wrong thing, didn't want to make things worse. But there was no avoiding this conversation. The silence between them was already unbearable.

With a shaky breath, Nocturne typed, *"I don't know if we can fix this. But I'll try. I'm ready to talk."*

It wasn't a promise of immediate resolution, but it was a start. It was a step toward acknowledging the hurt they'd both caused. And for now, that was enough.

59

CHAPTER NINE

FRAGILE THREADS

The fragile threads that had once bound them together now felt stretched and frayed, their edges raw and uncertain, barely holding on. The silence between them, though unspoken, was deafening—a chasm filled with memories, regret, and the things they had been too afraid to say. And yet, despite the weight of all that had passed between them, there was something undeniable, something that refused to let go: a connection that, though weakened, was still there, clinging desperately to the remnants of the friendship they had once fought so hard to protect.

The trio had not seen each other since the night the curse was lifted. That night had changed everything, not just for Nocturne, but for all of them. The ritual, the sheer desperation in their voices, the fear that had clawed at their insides as they stood on the brink of something irreversible—it had all left an imprint on them, carving deep wounds that had yet to heal. And in the aftermath, instead of coming together, they had let the silence grow between them, letting uncertainty and doubt take root where trust had once thrived. Reznor had tried, in her own way, to hold things together, to pretend that they weren't drifting apart, but no matter how much she reached out, the distance only seemed to grow. The stolen glances, the unanswered messages, the way their conversations—once effortless—had become stilted and cautious, all of it was unbearable.

She knew things couldn't go on like this. They couldn't keep tiptoeing around each other, pretending that the fractures in their friendship weren't deepening with each passing day. They had fought too hard, had suffered too much together, to let it all slip away now. Nocturne needed to face the fear she wasn't willing to name—the fear that, now that the curse was gone, she no longer had a place in their lives. Hamoudi needed to acknowledge the anger and guilt that had made him lash out, the emotions he had buried instead of confronting. And Reznor—well, she needed to stop carrying it all on her shoulders alone. She needed to stop being the glue that held them together and start allowing herself to be vulnerable too.

So she had done the only thing she could think of: she had asked them to meet at their usual café. The café was called Edelweiss & Ash, a small, tucked-away sanctuary nestled between towering buildings, its warm glow a comforting contrast to the dreary gray of the rain outside. It had been their place for long—where they had huddled over steaming mugs in the winter, where they had whispered secrets and made promises they never thought they'd break. A place that had once felt like home, but now felt distant, unfamiliar, like a book left open too long, its story interrupted mid-sentence.

Reznor arrived first, shaking off the damp chill of the rain as she stepped inside, the familiar scent of coffee, cinnamon, and aged books wrapping around her like a worn-out embrace. The café was nearly empty at this hour, the usual hum of conversation reduced to the occasional clink of porcelain and the low, comforting sound of soft jazz humming from the old record player in the corner.

Behind the counter stood Madame Lillian, the café's owner—a sweet old woman with silver-streaked hair tied in a loose bun, eyes warm and wise like she had seen a thousand lifetimes pass through these walls. She had always had a soft spot for Reznor and her friends, often sneaking them extra pastries when they spent late evenings studying, laughing, and existing in the kind of easy harmony that felt impossible now.

Madame Lillian looked up as Reznor approached the counter, her wrinkled face breaking into a gentle smile. "Ah, my little storm cloud," she greeted, using the nickname she had given Reznor years ago. "It's been a while. I was starting to wonder if you three had found another café to haunt."

Reznor's throat tightened at that—you three. It used to be so natural, so effortless. She tried to smile, but it felt weak, unconvincing, like a mask that no longer fit her face. "No, we just... life got in the way, I guess," she murmured, wrapping her hands around the edge of the counter, needing something to hold onto.

Madame Lillian studied her for a long moment, the way her shoulders were tense, the way her eyes flickered toward their usual table—the one that had remained empty for weeks now. Then, with the kind of understanding that only came with age, she reached over and patted Reznor's hand gently.

"They're coming, aren't they?" she asked, not in an intrusive way, but in the way someone does when they already know the answer.

Reznor swallowed hard and nodded. "Yeah. I asked them to meet me here."

Madame Lillian smiled knowingly and turned to grab a small plate, placing one of her homemade almond cookies on it—Nocturne's favorite. "Friendships bend, but they don't break so easily," she said, sliding the plate toward Reznor. "You three have been through too much for this to be the end of your story."

Reznor wanted to believe that, wanted to hold onto the warmth in Madame Lillian's voice and let it fill the spaces where doubt had settled. But the past few weeks had made it hard to be hopeful. She sighed, shaking her head slightly. "I don't know, Lillian. It just feels... different now."

Madame Lillian tilted her head slightly, as if considering her words carefully. "Of course, it does. You've all been hurt, shaken. Change is scary, dear. But true friends?" She reached out, gently tucking a stray lock of Reznor's hair behind her ear, the way a grandmother might. "True friends never leave. They may stumble, may drift, may get lost for a while, but if the bond is real, they always find their way back."

Reznor blinked rapidly, forcing down the unexpected sting behind her eyes. She wanted to say something, to find the right words to express the storm of emotions swirling inside her, but all she could do was nod, her fingers tightening around the edge of the counter.

Madame Lillian smiled, as if she understood anyway. "Go sit, my dear. Breathe. And when they come, just talk. Sometimes, that's all it takes to start healing."

Reznor let out a slow breath, forcing herself to believe in the old woman's words. She took the plate of cookies and walked back to their table—their table—sitting down with her cup of jasmine tea and waiting, hoping, that tonight would be the night they found their way back to each other. Here, in the dim glow of warm lights, with the steady hum of soft music and the rich scent of coffee and freshly baked pastries lingering in the air, she hoped they could find some semblance of honesty. No distractions, no outside world. Just them. Just their emotions, raw and vulnerable, laid bare at last.

When the bell above the door chimed, signaling someone's arrival, Reznor's breath caught. She looked up just in time to see Hamoudi walk in first, shaking the raindrops from his jacket, his eyes scanning the room before they landed on her. There was hesitation in his step, a wariness in his expression that made something ache deep inside her chest. He approached slowly, slipping into the seat across from her, his fingers immediately moving to the menu even though Reznor knew he already had a preferred order.

"Hey," he murmured, his voice quieter than usual, lacking its usual warmth. He didn't meet her eyes right away, instead focusing on the laminated page in his hands. After a brief pause, he sighed and set it down. "I'll have a black coffee. No sugar."

The order wasn't surprising—Hamoudi always drank his coffee that way, strong and bitter, but something about the simplicity of the request made it feel heavier, as if he were clinging to some kind of stability in the midst of everything that felt uncertain.

A moment later, the door opened again, and Nocturne stepped inside. Her presence was quieter, more cautious than it had once been, but Reznor could still see the way her shoulders tensed, the way her eyes flickered around the café as though expecting judgment to lurk in the shadows. Her damp hair clung to the edges of her face, the dark strands framing eyes that held something unreadable—something guarded. When she finally approached, she offered a small, tight-lipped smile, one that didn't quite reach her eyes.

"Hi," she said simply before sinking into the seat beside Hamoudi.

She didn't reach for the menu. Instead, she leaned forward slightly, clasping her hands together, her fingers restless, fidgeting with the rings she always wore. It was a habit she had when she was nervous, and Reznor recognized it immediately.

After a long pause, Nocturne finally spoke again, her voice barely above a whisper. "I'll have an Earl Grey."

Reznor watched as the waitress nodded and walked away, leaving the three of them in thick, suffocating silence. She glanced between them, taking in the way Hamoudi kept his gaze downcast, his fingers tapping restlessly against his coffee cup, the way Nocturne's lips pressed together, as if she were biting back words she wasn't sure she was ready to say.

The tension was unbearable.

Taking a deep breath, Reznor forced herself to speak, her voice steady despite the storm raging inside her. "I think we need to talk," she said, each word measured, careful, heavy with meaning. "About everything. The curse, the anger, the silence. We can't keep pretending like everything's fine when it's not."

Hamoudi's jaw tensed, his grip tightening around his coffee cup, but he said nothing. Nocturne, too, looked away, her lips twitching downward in a frown, her fingers still fidgeting with her rings. It was clear that neither of them wanted to be the first to break the silence, the first to admit just how much had changed, just how much they had lost in the space between that night and now.

But Reznor knew that if they didn't face it now, if they kept running from the pain, from each other, then whatever remained of their friendship would slip away completely.

And that was something she simply could not allow.

"We've been avoiding this for too long. I know it's uncomfortable, but we need to face it," she continued. "The curse is gone, but there's so much more to deal with than just that. We have to confront what happened—the things we've said, the things we've felt, the things we've kept inside."

Nocturne's eyes flickered to Reznor, then quickly away, but there was something softer in her expression now, as if she were finally hearing the truth in Reznor's words.

"I know I've been distant," Nocturne said quietly, her voice tinged with the uncertainty that had been gnawing at her since the curse had been lifted. "I've just... I don't know who I am anymore. I mean, the curse defined me for so long, it was like everything in my life revolved around it. And now... I don't know what to do with myself. I feel like I'm floating in space, like I'm not even sure if I fit anywhere anymore."

Her voice cracked slightly as she spoke, the raw emotion slipping out before she could stop it. Reznor's heart twisted in her chest as she watched Nocturne struggle with her own vulnerability. She had always been strong—stoic, guarded—but now, her fear and doubt were palpable.

"You're not alone in this," Reznor said, her voice soft but firm. "You're not defined by the curse anymore. You're still the same person you were before it, Nocturne. You always have been. The only difference now is that you get to decide who you are, what you want to be."

Nocturne looked at her, her eyes searching, but the flicker of hope in Reznor's words seemed to settle something in her chest. She nodded slowly, her shoulders loosening just slightly. It wasn't an instant transformation, but it was a beginning. "I just wish I could believe that," she murmured.

Hamoudi shifted uncomfortably in his seat, his fingers tapping lightly on the rim of his cup. "It's not just you, Nocturne," he spoke up, his voice rough. "I've been a mess, too. I... I lashed out at you, and I'm sorry for that. I was so scared, so damn scared of losing you. I thought if I could just... control the situation, if I could just stop the curse from taking you away, then everything would be okay. But I was wrong. And I hurt you because of it. I'm sorry."

The sincerity in his voice hit Nocturne like a physical blow, and for a moment, the tears she had been holding back threatened to spill. She had been so hurt by his words—the accusation that it was all her fault—but hearing him admit that it wasn't her fault, that it was his own fear that had caused him to lash out, softened the sharp edges of her pain.

"I know you didn't mean it like that," she said quietly, her voice trembling slightly. "I just... I was so lost. I didn't know how to fix it, either. I didn't know how to make it all go away. But I see now that we're both just... scared. I'm scared, too. I'm scared of being alone again, of being abandoned. I've felt that way my whole life, and I just... I couldn't handle it anymore."

The vulnerability in Nocturne's admission hung in the air, and Reznor felt a pang of sadness for the girl who had carried the weight of the world on her shoulders for so long. Nocturne had always been the quiet one, the one who kept to herself, who rarely let anyone see how much pain she was in. But now, in this moment, she had opened up, allowed herself to be seen in a way that was raw, honest, and incredibly brave.

Hamoudi, for his part, didn't say anything. Instead, he reached across the table and placed his hand on Nocturne's, offering a silent, supportive gesture. She looked at his hand for a moment, then up at his face, and a small but genuine smile tugged at her lips.

Reznor, watching the two of them, felt a quiet sense of relief settle over her chest. They were starting to understand each other again. They were beginning to rebuild.

"I think we've all been carrying something we didn't know how to deal with," Reznor said quietly. "I've been trying to hold everything together—keep us all in one piece. But I can't do it alone. I need both of you. And I think we need each other, too."

Nocturne nodded, the corners of her mouth curving up just slightly. "We've always been a team, haven't we?" she said, her voice soft.

Hamoudi smiled faintly, his gaze meeting hers. "Yeah. And we still are."

The weight between them had lifted, if only slightly, like the first break in storm clouds after a long and merciless downpour. It wasn't gone—not entirely. The hurt, the unsaid words, the scars of everything they had been through still lingered in the spaces between them, silent but present. But there was something new now, something that hadn't been there in a long time. A willingness. A quiet, fragile hope.

They had talked, halting and hesitant at first, but then with more honesty than they had allowed themselves in weeks. The pain was still raw, the wounds still fresh, but they weren't looking away from them anymore. They weren't running.

As the last sips of tea and coffee were taken, the three of them sat in the comfortable hush of Edelweiss & Ash, the café that had once been their safe haven. And maybe—just maybe—it could be that again.

Reznor glanced at Nocturne, who was absently tracing the rim of her empty cup, her expression softer than it had been in weeks. There was something lighter in her eyes, something hesitant but genuine, as though she was finally allowing herself to believe she wasn't alone.

Hamoudi exhaled slowly, rubbing a hand over his face before leaning back in his chair. "That was... exhausting," he muttered, but there was no edge to his voice this time. Just weariness. Just truth.

Nocturne let out a quiet laugh, barely more than a breath, but it was real. "Yeah. But good."

Reznor smiled then, a small thing, barely noticeable—but real, like a flicker of warmth in the cold. "Yeah," she echoed, feeling the word settle in her chest.

It wasn't perfect. It wasn't easy. There were still pieces to pick up, still fractures that might take time to mend, still old wounds that might ache unexpectedly on the hardest of nights. But they weren't alone in it anymore. They were beginning again, slowly, one fragile thread at a time, stitching themselves back together with careful hands and cautious hearts.

And for now—for this quiet, fleeting moment beneath the dim café lights, with the scent of jasmine and coffee lingering in the air and the steady rhythm of rain against the windows—that was enough.

CHAPTER TEN

HORIZONS UNFOLDING

The semester was drawing to a close, and with it came an undercurrent of tension that clung to the very walls of Blackthorne High—a peculiar blend of exhaustion, excitement, and the bittersweet realization that yet another chapter was ending. The once-crowded hallways, usually filled with laughter, whispered gossip, and the careless confidence of youth, now bore witness to weary students dragging their feet, their faces shadowed by sleepless nights spent cramming for exams and rushing to complete last-minute assignments. Some thrived in this chaos, their adrenaline carrying them through the final stretch with an almost feverish energy. Others moved with a kind of quiet resignation, simply waiting for it all to be over, eager to shed the weight of textbooks, early mornings, and the ever-present pressure to succeed.

For some, this was just another checkpoint in the relentless cycle of academia—a hurdle to cross before diving back into the same familiar rhythm when the next term rolled around. For others, this was an ending in every sense of the word, the close of a significant chapter, filled with the unspoken knowledge that life beyond these walls would never quite be the same again.

For Reznor, it was both.

She sat alone in the dimly lit library, the glow of an old brass lamp casting flickering shadows across the table as she absently flipped through the worn pages of her notebook. The ink, smudged from the weight of her hand pressing against it night after night, held half-formed thoughts, fragments of poems, sketches of things she couldn't quite describe in words, and snippets of conversations that had once seemed too important to forget. This notebook had been her anchor, the one place where she had allowed herself to be unfiltered, where she had spilled her thoughts in moments of both clarity and chaos.

And now, as she sat there with the clock ticking steadily toward an inevitable future, she found herself staring at its pages, realizing just how much she had poured into these words—how much of herself had been shaped within these walls. Blackthorne High had been her battlefield, her sanctuary, and at times, her prison. It had seen her at her best and at her absolute worst. It had been the place where friendships were formed and fractured, where love had bloomed and faded, where she had fought battles that no one else had seen, and where she had learned, in her own quiet way, how to survive.

And now, she was supposed to walk away from it all.

She wasn't sure how she felt about that.

Across the table, her phone buzzed softly, breaking the silence, and she glanced at the screen. A message from Nocturne.

Thinking of hitting a festival this summer. Might spend some time up in the mountains too. Need the quiet.

Nocturne had always been like that—balancing between chaos and solitude, a wildfire that burned bright and hot but always sought the calm after the storm. Reznor could already picture her there, disappearing into the sea of a music festival crowd, the neon lights reflecting in her dark eyes, only to retreat days later to a secluded cabin somewhere, letting the echoes of the world fade into silence.

Hamoudi, on the other hand, had been talking about summer internships, though he had yet to fully commit to one. He was careful like that—always weighing his options, thinking two steps ahead. Reznor had a feeling that, deep down, he was just as uncertain about what came next as she was. Maybe that was why he hesitated.

And then there was her.

She could already feel it—that gnawing restlessness creeping in, the thought of staying still for too long sending an uncomfortable shiver through her. She knew she couldn't do it. She couldn't just sit back and wait for life to happen to her. The idea of spending another summer following the same routines, walking the same streets, trapped in the predictability of it all, made her feel like she was suffocating.

She needed a break. A reset. A way to shake off the weight of everything that had happened and step into something—anything—that felt different.

She just didn't know what that something was yet.

Elvira had been one of the few constants in Reznor's life lately, a grounding presence amidst all the uncertainty, the emotional turbulence, and the ever-growing sense that something in her life was shifting—changing in ways she couldn't yet fully understand. No matter how much time passed, no matter how many friendships had fractured or faded into the background, Elvira had remained, steady and unshaken, as if she could see through the storm raging inside Reznor's mind and had simply decided that she wasn't going anywhere.

So it was fitting, almost inevitable, that on the night finals had officially wrapped up and the suffocating weight of academia had finally begun to ease, they found themselves at Obsidian Veil, their usual haunt—a place that felt more like home than anywhere else ever had. The dark-lit goth club was a sanctuary for those who thrived in the shadows, where the air was thick with the deep, reverberating pulse of industrial basslines, the ghostly trails of cigarette smoke curling into the dimly glowing chandeliers, and the lingering scent of spilled whiskey mixed with aged leather. The walls, lined with crimson velvet and intricate gothic tapestries, seemed to breathe in time with the music, flickering candlelight casting elongated shadows across the sea of black-clad figures moving in hypnotic synchrony on the dance floor below. It was a place untouched by time, a place where the outside world didn't exist, where it didn't matter what had happened yesterday or what was waiting for them tomorrow—only the present moment, suspended in a haze of flickering lights and heart-thudding beats.

Elvira leaned lazily against the bar, one arm draped over the polished surface while the other clutched a worn sketchbook, her fingers idly tracing invisible patterns along its cover. She was watching the crowd with that same knowing smirk she always wore, the one that made it seem like she had already predicted how the night would unfold, like she was two steps ahead of everyone else in the room.

She turned to Reznor, amusement flickering in her dark eyes. "You're brooding again, Mortimer," she teased, nudging her lightly with her elbow, a playful challenge laced beneath her words.

Reznor, who had been staring absently into the depths of her drink, rolled her eyes, though the ghost of a smile tugged at the corners of her lips. "I'm thinking," she countered, the weight of her thoughts pressing down on her even as she tried to shake them off.

Elvira let out a knowing hum, shifting to face her more fully. "Uh-huh. And when you start 'thinking,' it usually means you're either about to write some long, dramatic existential monologue in that notebook of yours or you're about to come up with some reckless idea that's going to drag us all into something wildly questionable." She tilted her head, watching her closely, amusement laced with genuine curiosity. "So, which is it this time?"

Reznor hesitated for a fraction of a second, her fingers tightening around the rim of her glass, as if steadying herself before taking the plunge. She had been carrying this thought around for days now, maybe even weeks, turning it over in her mind, feeling it grow and take shape until it was no longer just a fleeting impulse but something more—something that had begun to feel inevitable.

She exhaled, finally setting her drink down with a quiet clink against the counter, before turning fully toward Elvira. "I want to leave for a bit," she said, her voice quieter, but firm, the weight of the words settling between them like a declaration. "I need to get out of here. I don't know... I just feel like I need something—air, distance, a change of scenery—just something different."

Elvira arched a perfectly shaped eyebrow, her fingers tapping against her sketchbook as she considered this revelation. "A vacation?" she asked, her tone casual, but there was something keen in the way she was studying Reznor now, as if she could already sense that this wasn't just some passing whim.

Reznor shook her head. "A road trip," she clarified, and for the first time in weeks—maybe even months—saying it out loud made it feel real.

Elvira's expression shifted, the teasing edge fading as something more thoughtful took its place. She didn't respond right away, just watched Reznor with a quiet intensity, as if weighing the weight of those words, as if she understood that this wasn't just about a trip—it was about something deeper, something unspoken, something restless that had been gnawing at Reznor for too long now.

And then, after a long pause, her lips curved into a slow, knowing grin, one that held none of the earlier amusement but something warmer, something that said she understood, maybe better than Reznor had expected.

"That," Elvira said, lifting her glass slightly in a silent toast, "is the best thing you've said in months."

It didn't take long for the idea to take root. In fact, once it had been spoken into existence, it grew rapidly, weaving itself into Reznor's mind like ivy creeping up the side of an abandoned house—wild, untamed, impossible to ignore.

By the next morning, she had already decided that she couldn't keep it to herself any longer. This wasn't just some passing whim, some fleeting urge that would dissolve under the weight of practicality. No, this was something different—something necessary. It was movement, escape, freedom. And deep down, she knew she wasn't the only one who needed it.

So, as the early afternoon sun cast long shadows across the cobblestone paths of Blackthorne High's campus, Reznor found Nocturne and Hamoudi in their usual spot—tucked away beneath the ancient willow tree that loomed near the edge of the courtyard, its sprawling branches shielding them from the world. It was a place of quiet, of familiarity, of whispered conversations and unspoken understandings. But today, it was going to be the birthplace of something new.

She wasted no time.

"A road trip," she announced, dropping onto the grass beside them, her words slicing through the comfortable silence like a blade. "Let's do it. Just us. No plans, no schedules, no expectations—just the open road and whatever comes next."

Nocturne, who had been lazily twirling a strand of her violet-streaked hair between her fingers, glanced up from her book with a skeptical arch of her brow. "A road trip? To where?" she asked, her tone laced with both amusement and doubt, as though she was still trying to figure out whether Reznor was joking or had, in fact, lost her mind entirely.

Reznor shrugged, leaning back on her elbows, her gaze drifting toward the sky. "Does it matter?" she countered, her voice carrying that familiar edge of defiance. "The whole point is to go. To move. To get the hell out of here for a while and just exist without all the bullshit dragging us down. No plans, no destination—just the road and whatever comes with it."

Hamoudi, ever the rational one, let out a slow breath, his brows knitting together as he considered the idea. "I don't know, Rez," he said, his voice cautious, measured. "That sounds... chaotic."

Reznor turned to him then, a slow grin spreading across her lips, the kind that meant she wasn't going to back down. "Good," she said simply, her eyes gleaming with something wild, something untamed.

For a moment, neither of them said anything. The weight of what she was proposing settled between them, thick and heavy, pressing against the uncertainty that had clung to their group like a second skin ever since the night the curse had been lifted.

And then, almost imperceptibly, something shifted.

Nocturne was the first to cave, exhaling a deep sigh before closing her book with a definitive thud. "Alright," she murmured, stretching her legs out in front of her. "Fine. But if we end up in some sketchy middle-of-nowhere gas station with a guy named Earl trying to sell us canned meat from 1998, I'm blaming you."

Reznor smirked. "Deal."

Hamoudi, though still clearly hesitant, ran a hand through his dark curls, his gaze flickering between the two of them before shaking his head with a reluctant chuckle. "God help us," he muttered. "Fine. I'm in. But if we get arrested, I'm telling them this was your idea."

"Noted," Reznor said, grinning as she reached for her phone. "Now, let's make this official."

By the time they settled into their usual corner at Edelweiss & Ash, the cozy little café they had claimed as their own over time, the road trip was no longer just an idea. It was a plan.

The scent of freshly brewed coffee and warm cinnamon lingered in the air, the soft hum of jazz playing from the antique record player tucked in the corner. The café's owner, Marguerite, had greeted them with her usual warm smile before disappearing behind the counter, leaving them to their quiet scheming.

Elvira, perched across from them, listened with an amused expression, her black-painted nails tapping rhythmically against the side of her ceramic mug. "So," she said at last, her lips curving into that slow, knowing smirk, "looks like you got your reckless idea, Mortimer."

Reznor clinked her own mug against hers, the soft chime ringing between them like an unspoken promise. "And you're coming with us," she said, tilting her head challengingly.

Elvira chuckled, taking a slow sip of her drink before setting it down with deliberate finality. "Wouldn't miss it."

And just like that, the wheels were set in motion.

They didn't know where they were going. They didn't know how long they'd be gone. They didn't know what they would find out there on the open road, what ghosts they might have to face, what truths they might uncover.

But for the first time in a long time, the uncertainty didn't feel like something to fear.

It felt exhilarating.

The road was calling.

And they were finally ready to answer.

The road stretched endlessly before them, a winding path cutting through rolling green hills and sunlit meadows, the horizon stretching far beyond the limits of their imagination. The car—a battered but beloved black sedan Elvira had sweet-talked a mechanic into fixing up last summer—moved like a shadow through the golden light of late afternoon, windows rolled down, music blasting from the speakers. The air smelled of warm earth and asphalt, a scent that carried the promise of adventure, of untold stories waiting to unfold.

The four of them—Reznor, Nocturne, Hamoudi, and Elvira—fit together in the car like mismatched puzzle pieces that somehow formed a perfect whole. The weight of everything they had been through still clung to them in fragments, but it felt lighter now, something they could finally breathe through rather than suffocate beneath.

"Did you see his face when I told him I wasn't interested in his lame excuses?" Reznor chuckled, shaking her head as she shot a glance at Nocturne in the passenger seat, who had her boots propped up on the dashboard, the wind whipping through her dark, violet-streaked hair.

Nocturne smirked, adjusting her sunglasses. "Priceless. You've got a talent for making people squirm, Reznor."

Hamoudi, stretched out in the backseat, feet propped up against the armrest, let out a low chuckle. "Yeah, but let's not forget who had to talk us out of getting kicked out of that café. Again."

"Details," Reznor waved a hand dismissively.

"You guys are so bad at staying out of trouble," Elvira quipped from the driver's seat, her fingers drumming lightly against the steering wheel. "I leave you alone for two minutes, and suddenly, there's an argument with a barista, and we're getting looks from the entire café."

"To be fair," Nocturne said, grinning, "Reznor didn't start it. She just... escalated it."

"And finished it," Reznor added with a self-satisfied smirk.

Elvira rolled her eyes but couldn't help the amused smile that tugged at her lips. She adjusted her grip on the wheel, her silver rings catching the sunlight as the car hummed along the open road. The trunk was packed with snacks, clothes they had barely folded, and a duffel bag full of things they would probably never need but brought anyway—because who knew what the road would throw at them?

This trip wasn't just a getaway. It was a reckoning, a declaration of victory against everything that had tried to break them.

Their destination? Cedar Shores—a quiet, secluded lakeside retreat they had all spoken about in passing over the years but never quite managed to visit. For Nocturne, it had been the setting of childhood dreams, a place untouched by fear or expectation. For Hamoudi, it was a reset button, a symbolic "start-over" point that they desperately needed. And for Reznor? She wasn't sure yet. Maybe she just wanted to see if freedom really felt as good as she imagined it would.

The music pulsed through the speakers, a carefully curated playlist of rock, goth, and metal tracks that perfectly matched the energy thrumming between them. Every now and then, one of them would belt out a chorus off-key, earning laughter and groans from the rest. They had nowhere to be, no deadlines, no ghosts clawing at their heels. Just miles of open road and the promise of something new.

And then Nocturne's phone buzzed in her lap.

She glanced at the screen, her breath catching slightly.

Elvira noticed first. "Everything okay?"

Nocturne hesitated for a beat before answering, her voice quieter than before. "It's my dad."

Reznor and Hamoudi exchanged a glance but didn't say anything. They knew better than to push her.

Nocturne exhaled and answered the call, her voice steady despite the emotions tightening in her chest. "Hello?"

A pause. Then, a voice—warm, hesitant. "Nocturne. I... I wanted to call and check on you. I heard about everything, and I—I just wanted to say that I'm proud of you."

The words hung in the air, heavier than she had expected.

For years, she had longed for this. For him to see her—not as the embodiment of the family's tragedies, not as the girl everyone whispered about, but as her. As Nocturne.

She swallowed, trying to steady herself. "Thank you," she said finally, her voice thick with emotion. "That means a lot."

"I was hoping," her father continued, his tone softer now, "that you might come visit. When you're ready, of course. I'd like to see you. To talk. Properly this time."

Nocturne's grip on the phone tightened.

For a moment, she didn't know what to say. But then, she glanced around the car—at Reznor, who was watching her carefully; at Hamoudi, who was pretending not to listen but clearly was; and at Elvira, whose eyes flicked toward the rearview mirror, catching Nocturne's gaze with quiet encouragement.

And suddenly, it didn't feel as terrifying as it once had.

"I'd like that," she said, her voice barely above a whisper.

When she hung up, she stared out the window for a long moment, watching as the rolling hills blurred into golden streaks under the setting sun. The wind caught the loose strands of her hair, whipping them around her face.

Reznor reached over, gave her hand a reassuring squeeze.

"You okay?"

Nocturne let out a slow breath. Then, for the first time in a long time, she smiled—not just a small, polite smile, but a real one. A hopeful one.

"Yeah," she said, her voice steady now. "I think I am."

Elvira reached forward, flicking up the volume on the stereo as their favorite song came on.

"Well then," she grinned, "let's keep driving."

And just like that, the road stretched on, infinite and untamed, welcoming them into the unknown.

By the time they arrived at Cedar Shores, the sun was beginning its slow descent, casting the vast lake in hues of gold and amber. The car rolled to a stop near the water's edge, and the four of them—Reznor, Nocturne, Hamoudi, and Elvira—piled out, stretching their legs after hours on the road. The air smelled of pine and earth, crisp and cool, carrying the faintest hint of summer's arrival. The lake stretched endlessly before them, its surface still as glass, reflecting the silhouette of towering trees and the burning sky above.

For a long moment, none of them spoke. They simply stood there, taking it all in, letting the weight of reality settle into their bones. This wasn't just some abstract dream anymore, some half-formed wish muttered over late-night conversations. They were here. The place that had only existed in stories and fragmented imaginings had finally become real.

Elvira, who had been quiet for most of the drive, let out a low whistle. "Damn," she murmured. "That's a view."

Nocturne exhaled, a small, contented smile tugging at her lips. "Better than I imagined."

Reznor tossed her duffel bag onto the sand, shaking out her stiff limbs. "Guess we didn't completely screw up our first road trip."

"You sound surprised," Hamoudi teased, chucking a small stone into the water, watching the ripples spread outward.

"Not surprised," Reznor said with a smirk. "Just impressed. We actually made it without anyone getting arrested, lost, or cursed. I'd call that progress."

They laughed, the sound easy and unburdened, before settling onto a wide blanket near the shoreline. They unpacked snacks, passing around chips and drinks as they soaked in the atmosphere. The tension that had followed them for months, the remnants of old fears and past demons, felt distant here—like ghosts left behind in the places they had outgrown.

It was Hamoudi who broke the comfortable silence first. He leaned back on his elbows, staring up at the sky as it deepened into dusky purples and oranges. "You know," he mused, "when I first met you three, I never thought we'd end up here."

Reznor, who had been absently tracing patterns in the sand, glanced up. "What, you didn't think we'd survive the curse?"

Hamoudi chuckled, shaking his head. "It's not that. I just didn't think I'd ever be part of something like this. I always kept people at arm's length, you know? I thought it was safer that way. Less mess, less risk. But you three—you've shown me that it's okay to let people in. That sometimes, it's worth it."

Elvira, sitting cross-legged beside him, nudged his shoulder playfully. "Sometimes? Wow, thanks, Hamoudi. Real heartwarming."

Hamoudi rolled his eyes. "Fine. Most of the time."

Nocturne smiled, the warmth in her expression rare but genuine. "You took a risk on us too, Hamoudi. And it means more than you know."

Reznor raised her bottle of soda in a mock toast. "To risks that pay off."

Elvira, grinning, grabbed her own bottle. "To not dying horribly in the process."

They clinked their bottles together, laughter bubbling up between them, loud and uninhibited.

As the sun dipped lower, the sky darkening into twilight, Reznor found herself staring out at the water, lost in thought. The past few months replayed in her mind like an old film reel—the fear, the doubt, the moments where it felt like everything was too much. But there had been light, too. Strength. The bond they had forged, the things they had survived, the parts of themselves they had reclaimed from the shadows.

"It's strange," she said, her voice cutting through the quiet. "Looking back on everything, it's like...the curse wasn't just about Nocturne. It was about all of us. The things we were afraid to face. The parts of ourselves we didn't want to see."

Nocturne nodded slowly, her gaze fixed on the rippling water. "It's like it forced us to confront the shadows we were carrying. And now... they're not so heavy anymore."

Hamoudi leaned back, staring at the first stars winking into the night sky. "That's the thing about shadows," he murmured. "They only exist because of the light."

Reznor turned to him, raising an eyebrow. "When did you get so poetic?"

He shrugged, smirking. "I hang out with you guys. It rubs off."

Elvira laughed softly, shaking her head. "I swear, if one of you starts reciting tragic poetry, I'm throwing you into the lake."

Reznor smirked. "Tempting, but too much effort."

As night fell, they lit a small campfire, the flickering flames casting long shadows around them. They shared stories, memories—some painful, some hilarious, all woven together with laughter. There was no heaviness in the air, no looming sense of dread. Just them, together, untethered, finally free.

At one point, Nocturne rose to her feet and wandered toward the water's edge. The firelight illuminated her silhouette, her reflection shimmering on the surface. She stared out at the horizon, her heart light in a way it hadn't been in years.

She thought about her father's words. About how the town had started looking at her differently—not with whispers or pitying glances, but with something else. Maybe even respect.

She thought about the future, about the possibilities stretching out before her. And for the first time, the unknown didn't seem daunting. It felt... exhilarating.

"I'm not cursed," she whispered, the words carried away by the gentle breeze. "I never was."

Behind her, the others stood, one by one.

Reznor, arms crossed, her voice firm. "No. You never were."

Hamoudi, standing beside her, nodding. "And you never will be."

Elvira, smirking, added, "We told you so."

Nocturne exhaled, closing her eyes for a brief moment before opening them again, looking out into the endless night. The stars reflected off the water, stretching infinitely in every direction.

For the first time, she believed it.

They stood together in silence for a long while, letting the moment settle, letting it mean something.

And as the first embers of dawn began to creep along the horizon, they knew—this wasn't the end.

It was only the beginning.

Epilogue: Eternal Bonds

The curse was gone. Truly, finally, gone. Yet for Reznor, Nocturne, and Hamoudi, the end of the darkness didn't mean their story was over—it was merely the beginning of something new, something brighter.

For Nocturne, life without the curse was like stepping into the sunlight for the first time. Her shoulders no longer sagged under the invisible weight that had burdened her for so long. Her laughter, once rare and subdued, became a regular part of her personality. Though she still wore her gothic aesthetic—lace gloves, flowing skirts, and dark chokers—it now seemed celebratory rather than sorrowful.

Hamoudi, steadfast as ever, was deeply affected by their journey. The trials they had faced awakened in him a sense of purpose, a need to build something lasting and meaningful. He began applying to architecture programs, determined to craft structures that could stand against time, much like their friendships.

Reznor, however, felt a quiet shift in herself that went beyond the physical act of breaking the curse. Her love for stories—both writing them and living them—deepened into a calling. She realized she wanted to take the experiences of her life and turn them into something others could connect to.

But while Nocturne and Hamoudi formed a new rhythm alongside Reznor, there was someone else who remained a constant in her life—Elvira. Known to the world as Veronica, Elvira was Reznor's first true friend and her most enduring connection outside the trio.

Elvira wasn't part of the trio's fight against the curse. She wasn't there during the rituals, nor did she experience the supernatural terrors firsthand. Yet, her influence on Reznor was no less profound. She had been the quiet foundation of their friendship, a steadfast presence that reminded Reznor of who she was beyond the chaos.

Their bond was unique, formed in whispered conversations under the flickering glow of neon signs, in shared playlists of obscure goth bands, and in the comfort of simply existing together without pretense. Where the trio represented adventure, challenge, and camaraderie, Elvira was something softer and more intimate—a mirror that reflected Reznor's inner self.

A month after the curse was broken, Reznor sat on the floor of Elvira's room, surrounded by the comforting chaos of her best friend's life. The walls were adorned with posters of The Sisters of Mercy and Bauhaus, and a record spun lazily on the player, filling the space with melancholic tunes.

"So," Elvira said, lounging on her bed with a sketchpad in hand. "How does it feel to be a curse-breaker?"

Reznor smiled, though her expression was tinged with weariness. "Relieved, mostly. But also... I don't know. Empty, I guess? Like, that whole ordeal defined my life for so long. Now that it's over, I'm not sure who I am without it."

Elvira paused her sketching and looked at her. "You're still you, Mortimer. You don't need a crisis to be interesting or worthy. You've always been enough."

Reznor blinked, caught off guard by the sincerity in Elvira's voice. "Thanks," she said softly.

Elvira smirked, the moment of tenderness quickly replaced by her usual sarcasm. "Of course, now you owe me. I expect at least three free copies of whatever brooding novel you write about this whole thing."

Several weeks later, Reznor, Nocturne, and Hamoudi gathered in the clearing where the curse had been broken. The forest, once shrouded in an oppressive atmosphere, felt lighter now. Sunlight filtered through the trees, illuminating the spot where they had stood united against the darkness.

"We should leave something here," Reznor suggested, breaking the reflective silence.

"Like what?" Nocturne asked, tilting her head.

"Something permanent," Reznor said. "To remind us of this moment, of everything we've been through."

Hamoudi nodded thoughtfully. "What about a tree? It'll grow, just like we did. It'll be here long after we're gone."

Nocturne smiled. "I like that idea. It feels... hopeful."

The following weekend, they returned with a young sapling, a shovel, and a sense of purpose. Together, they dug a hole in the center of the clearing and planted the tree. As they stood back to admire their work, Reznor felt a deep sense of closure.

"This tree is us," she said, her voice steady. "It's our strength, our growth, our future."

Hamoudi placed a hand on the trunk, his expression serious. "Here's to us," he said. "To everything we've overcome—and everything that's still ahead."

Nocturne and Reznor joined him, their hands resting on the tree. For a moment, they stood in silence, their bond unspoken but undeniable.

While the trio's bond remained unshakable, Reznor continued to nurture her friendship with Elvira. They met often, usually in Elvira's art-filled room or at the dimly lit café downtown.

One evening, as they sat across from each other at their favorite café, Reznor told Elvira about the tree.

"It's in the clearing," Reznor said, her eyes lighting up as she spoke. "The place where it all happened. It's small now, but one day it'll be huge. It's a symbol of everything we've been through."

Elvira smiled, stirring her coffee. "Sounds like a goth fairytale. I'd love to see it."

"We should go," Reznor said. "It feels right, showing it to you."

A few months later, Reznor and Elvira visited the clearing together. The sapling had grown taller, its branches reaching upward with quiet determination.

"It's beautiful," Elvira said, her voice soft.

Reznor nodded, a sense of pride swelling in her chest. "It's more than a tree. It's us."

They sat beneath its growing canopy, their conversation drifting between the past, the present, and the future. Elvira sketched the tree in her notebook, her strokes capturing its essence in a way words never could.

"Do you ever think about what life would've been like if none of this had happened?" Reznor asked, her gaze distant.

Elvira paused, considering the question. "Sometimes. But I think it all happened the way it was supposed to. Even the dark stuff. It brought you to where you are now."

Reznor smiled. "You're annoyingly wise, you know that?"

Elvira smirked. "Someone has to be."

As the years passed, life carried each of them in different directions. Reznor became a published author, her stories deeply influenced by the journey she had shared with Nocturne, Hamoudi, and even Elvira. Her debut novel, Shadows of the Clearing, became a bestseller, resonating with readers who saw their own struggles reflected in its pages.

Nocturne pursued a career in psychology, her understanding of darkness and resilience making her an extraordinary therapist. She often spoke about the importance of connection and the strength that came from facing fears head-on.

Hamoudi excelled in architecture, his designs blending modernity with nature. He often returned to the clearing, sketching the now-mature tree and drawing inspiration from its enduring presence.

Elvira's art gained recognition far beyond their hometown. Her pieces, often themed around resilience and transformation, became a source of healing for others. Though their lives were busy, she and Reznor remained as close as ever, their friendship a constant amid the changes.

The years passed. Seasons turned, friendships evolved, and the tree grew. It became a place of pilgrimage—not just for the trio but for others who stumbled upon it, drawn by its quiet strength. The names carved into its trunk—Reznor, Nocturne, Hamoudi, and eventually Elvira—stood as a testament to what had been endured and overcome.

One autumn evening, decades after planting the tree, Reznor returned to the clearing alone. She was older now, her hands marked by time and her hair streaked with silver, but the fire in her eyes remained. The tree was massive, its branches stretching out like an embrace, its roots visible above the soil, as if the earth itself couldn't contain its growth.

She ran her hand over its rough bark, her fingers brushing against the names carved into its trunk.

"It's been a long time," she murmured, her voice carried away by the wind.

A group of children playing in the forest stumbled upon her, their laughter fading as they entered the quiet clearing. They stopped a few feet away, staring up at the massive tree with wide, curious eyes. Its branches stretched high and wide, casting long shadows in the late afternoon light. The carved names on its trunk caught their attention, etched deep and weathered with age.

"Who were they?" one of the children asked, pointing at the names. Their voice was small but clear, carrying the kind of innocent curiosity only a child could muster.

Reznor turned toward them, startled at first by their presence but quickly softening. She smiled, her expression warm and wistful, as if she were speaking to someone from her own past. "They were friends," she said gently, her voice steady despite the flood of memories threatening to overwhelm her. "They faced something dark, something terrifying, but they stuck together. They found their strength in each other."

The children leaned closer, their faces lit with awe. "And this tree? Did they plant it?" another child asked, their fingers grazing the rough bark as if it might whisper secrets to them.

Reznor nodded slowly, her hand resting lightly on the tree's trunk. "Yes. This tree is because of them. It's a reminder—to me, to you, to everyone—that no matter how hard things get, no matter how impossible it feels, we're stronger when we stand together. When we choose hope. When we grow."

The children stared at her, solemn and thoughtful in the way children rarely were, absorbing her words. Then, as quickly as they had appeared, their curiosity gave way to the pull of their game. With small nods of understanding, they scampered off, their laughter ringing out as they disappeared back into the forest.

Reznor remained, her gaze following them until they were gone, leaving her once again in the stillness of the clearing. She lowered herself to the base of the tree, leaning against its sturdy trunk as she let her fingers trace the grooves of the carved names. Her own name, Reznor, sat next to Nocturne's, Hamoudi's, and Elvira's, each mark a testament to their bond. It was strange to think how small they had been when they carved those letters, their hands trembling from exhaustion but filled with determination to leave a piece of themselves here.

Her head tilted back against the bark, and her eyes fluttered shut. The memories came in waves now, unbidden but welcome, wrapping around her like an old, familiar quilt. She thought of Nocturne—her sharp wit, her quiet strength, and the way her laughter, once so rare, had blossomed in the years after the curse was broken. Nocturne had faced her demons and risen, choosing to channel her pain into helping others find their own light. Reznor smiled faintly, imagining her friend now, her voice steady and comforting as she guided someone else out of the shadows.

Then there was Hamoudi, ever the steadying force, the one who never wavered in his belief that they could overcome anything as long as they stood together. His passion for building—whether it was relationships, dreams, or the literal structures he designed—had taken him far. Yet he always returned to the clearing, sketchpad in hand, drawing inspiration from this very tree. Reznor could still hear his voice, steady and full of conviction, saying, "This tree is us. It's everything we've been through, and everything we still can be."

And then there was Elvira. Elvira, who had never stood in the clearing during the curse's darkest moments but had always been a part of Reznor's story. Her quiet presence, her sarcastic humor, her unwavering belief in Reznor's worth—they had been Reznor's anchor. Elvira hadn't needed to fight the darkness to be a hero. She had fought for Reznor simply by staying, by being. And even after all these years, that bond had never frayed. Elvira's art—her way of capturing emotion and resilience—still hung in Reznor's home, a daily reminder of the friend who had always seen her for who she truly was.

Reznor's fingers tightened slightly against the bark, her throat constricting as a swell of emotion rose within her. She thought of the nights they had spent here, the fear and exhaustion they had shared, the way they had clung to one another when it felt like the darkness might swallow them whole. They had been broken, scared, and unsure—but they had survived. Together, they had chosen hope when it would have been easier to give in. And that choice had changed everything.

The tree before her was no longer just a symbol; it was a monument to the kind of love and friendship that could outlast even the heaviest storms. Its roots were deep, unshakable, just like the bonds they had forged. Its branches stretched skyward, reaching for the light, a testament to their growth and resilience. And though time had carried them in different directions, the tree stood as proof that they had lived, that they had endured, and that they had mattered.

As the sun dipped lower, casting the clearing in a warm, golden light, Reznor whispered into the quiet, her voice soft but full of meaning. "Thank you," she said, her words meant for the tree, for the clearing, for the friends who had shaped her life. "For everything."

The wind rustled through the leaves, as if carrying her gratitude into the ether, spreading it to the ones who could no longer stand beside her in person but who would forever remain in her heart.

She stayed there until the light faded, until the clearing was bathed in the cool tones of twilight. When she finally rose, brushing leaves from her coat, she turned to the tree one last time, her gaze lingering on the carved names. Her fingers brushed the bark as though she could feel the essence of her friends through it.

As she walked away, the clearing grew still once more, the tree standing tall and proud against the backdrop of the fading sky. It had witnessed their struggles, their triumphs, and their growth, and it would continue to stand as a silent reminder of what they had overcome.

For Reznor, the tree wasn't just a reminder of the past. It was a promise—a testament to resilience, love, and the enduring power of friendship. A piece of her heart would always remain in this clearing, beneath the shade of its branches, where a group of friends had once stood together and chosen to fight for the light.

Bibliography

The following sources inspired or supported the creation of this work:

Books and Literature

Gothic Tales: An Anthology – A collection of gothic literature that deeply influenced the setting, atmosphere, and themes of *Cursed Bonds*.

Myths, Magic, and the Occult by A. J. Cartwright – A comprehensive guide to understanding historical witchcraft, folklore, and the evolution of magical traditions.

The Language of Curses and Spells by Miriam Solis – A study of the symbolic and historical significance of magical rituals and incantations.

Shadows and Light: Exploring Gothic Themes in Literature by Thomas Abernathy – A critical analysis that informed the gothic tone of the story.

Bloodlines: The History of Family Curses by Evelyn Marks – A fascinating exploration of generational curses in folklore and their cultural significance.

The Art of Gothic Storytelling by L. H. Turner – A practical guide for crafting gothic fiction that influenced the structure of *Cursed Bonds*.

Historical and Cultural References

The Witch Trials of Europe by Karen Blackwell – Provided historical context for Marguerite Delacroix's backstory and the persecution of witches in the gothic era.

Dark Pacts and Ancient Deals by Victor Hale – An exploration of mythical and historical pacts with supernatural entities, which inspired the central curse in the novel.

Psychology and Human Behavior

The Shadow Self: Understanding Our Darkest Aspects by Dr. Caroline Foster – A psychological perspective on the darker sides of human nature, reflected in Nocturne's struggles.

The Resilient Mind by Dr. Ayesha Khan – Insights into mental resilience, which influenced the portrayal of Nocturne's emotional journey.

Folklore and Mythology

Witchcraft Through the Ages by Tobias Crane – A historical account of witchcraft practices and beliefs that informed Marguerite's character.

Serpents in Mythology and Magic by Sophia Rayner – A detailed analysis of serpentine imagery, which is central to the curse's symbolism.

The Veil Between Worlds by Dr. Edward Hawthorne – A study of the concept of liminal spaces and their significance in supernatural lore.

Inspirations from Other Media

Classic gothic novels like **Mary Shelley's** *Frankenstein* and **Bram Stoker's** *Dracula* inspired the eerie, mysterious tone of the story.

The music of artists such as **Nine Inch Nails**, Double Eyelid, **Evanescence**, and **Lana Del Rey**, whose haunting melodies and lyrics informed the emotional depth of the narrative.

Personal Research and Observations

Journals and family heirlooms provided inspiration for the discovery of Marguerite's story in the attic scene.

BIBLIOGRAPHY

Conversations with historians and folklore experts contributed to the authenticity of the historical elements.

Personal reflections on resilience, friendships, and self-discovery shaped the core emotional journey of the protagonist.

About The Author

Riya Mattoos is a writer with a background in forensic science and applied psychology, specializing in clinical and counseling psychology. With a keen interest in human behavior and a passion for exploring the darker sides of the human experience, Riya's debut novel, *Cursed Bonds: A Fate Entwined*, is an emotional journey of resilience, self-discovery, and the complexities of friendship.

At 25 years old, Riya has recently completed her studies and is now navigating the exciting yet uncertain path of figuring out life. Along the way, she is pursuing her love for writing, art, and other creative outlets that allow her to express the complexity of emotions and experiences. Her love for the gothic lifestyle—its deep, mysterious, and often melancholic elements—greatly influences her creative work. Additionally, Riya is passionate about acting and movies, drawing inspiration from cinematic storytelling to enhance her own narrative style.

When she's not writing, Riya enjoys immersing herself in classic literature, experimenting with art, and exploring music that speaks to her soul. *Cursed Bonds: A Fate Entwined* marks her first step into the world of storytelling, and she hopes readers connect with its themes as deeply as she did while writing it.